The Magician

By Keri A. Kovacsiss
and Lea M. Kovacsiss

The Magician

By Keri A. Kovacsiss and Lea M. Kovacsiss
Copyright © 2024 Keri A. Kovacsiss and Lea M. Kovacsiss

All rights reserved. No part of this publication may be reproduced, distributed, or transmitted in any form or by any means, or stored in a database or retrieval system, without prior written permission of the authors.

The scanning, uploading, and distribution of this book via the Internet or via other means without the permission of the publisher is illegal and punishable by law. Please purchase only authorized electronic editions, and do not participate in or encourage electronic piracy of copyrighted materials. Your support of the authors' rights is appreciated.

This is a work of fiction. Names, characters, places, and incidents are either the product of the authors' imaginations or are used fictitiously. Any resemblance to actual persons, living or dead, events, or locales, is purely coincidental.

Cover design: Pace Studios
ISBN: 979-8-9866326-2-9

Dedication

This book is dedicated in loving memory to our dear friends, Joe Hoag, Sr., and Rosemary Rodgers. You are forever in our hearts.

Contents

Chapter 1 1

Chapter 2 27

Chapter 3 53

Chapter 4 71

Chapter 5 91

Chapter 6 115

Chapter 7 139

Chapter 8 163

Chapter 9 187

Chapter 10 211

Acknowledgments

First and foremost, we would like to thank our partners, Ryan McAuley and David Yang, our incredible parents, Bob and Tami Kovacsiss, grandmother, Patricia Kovacsiss, sister, Jamie Ickes, and larger family. This project would not be a reality without your constant support and encouragement. To our editors Mark Hanigan and Jenny Spencer: we can't thank you enough for joining us on the second part of this journey. To Amanda Riley and Kristin Rodgers: thank you for your constant support and feedback. To Maria Licodo Pace: thank you for your dedication to this project. Your involvement means the world to us.

Chapter 1

The tourists were gone, the excitement was gone, and now I had to deal with myself. I began to realize clutter could serve a purpose. If you cluttered up your life, you did not have to deal with yourself. And I certainly did not want to deal with myself, deal with the events of last year—deal with, potentially, the truth about my family.

I pictured myself at the edge of a black hole, steeling myself from falling straight into the abyss. I wanted to confront my life, my history; I wanted to "dive-in." I wanted to know. I did. But I also wanted to back away, fill in the hole, and put a stone lid firmly over it, never to be explored again.

However, relics of the past were never truly sealed away. I had watched enough of the *History Channel* to know; relics could easily be uncovered. One shift and there they were: exposed. I felt the shift already, a movement so slight it was almost imperceptible, but still there, nonetheless. I knew it was time to confront the truth, whatever the truth may be.

The holidays passed in a whirlwind, and we did it all. We carved the turkey; we ate the pie. We burned the Yule log; we exchanged the gifts. We even attended a New Year's Eve party where we tasted miniature cakes—lemon, carrot, red velvet, and chocolate—along with glasses full of bubbly pink champagne. While I enjoyed myself, I never felt truly there.

Everything felt slowed, dimmed. There would be moments where I could almost reach joy, and yet it hung just out of my emotional reach. I realize now that I was grateful for the chaotic time. There was always a distraction, always something going on.

My older sister Theodora seemed to conjure up endless tasks for my younger sister Tara and me to complete. We cleaned, decorated, baked, and canned. We even prepped for the Spring Ostara Festival, which we almost never did during the crazy holiday season. If I did not know better, I would think she was trying to keep me busy. All I wanted to do was lie in bed.

"You have to get up," Theo said one morning, staring down at me curled up on the couch in my sitting room, a blanket over me. She threw open the newly purchased curtains to my balcony, unveiling the view that I once swore that I would never cover, letting the sunlight shine into the room. Darkness was my friend now, allowing for sleep well after the sun came up. It was some time after New Year's Day, and the weather was as dreadful as I felt inside: bitter, cold, with no sign of thawing.

I pulled the blanket over my head, defiant.

"I've made a lot of allowances for you, Treasure. If you do not want to... you know... go to the police station again... then fine. But you can't lay around all day while everyone else takes care of you."

I said nothing. I did not want to address the whole Mills "thing" or the Jimmy Dickson "thing" or the Mrs. VanHoy "thing." Since last year's All Hallows' Eve Parade and Pageant, my life had been turned upside down. Every year, Seven Hills, Massachusetts, the little town in which I grew up and still resided, threw what could only be described as an All Hallows' Eve extravaganza. Seven Hills, a historical town, is famous for their "witch trials." Five women were tried and hanged as witches, in downtown Seven Hills, in the late 1600s. In more current times, the All Hallows' Eve Parade and Pageant served to honor and celebrate the women's legacy—as well as to attract tourists, allowing the town to financially stay afloat. The tourism certainly helped me and my sisters' business: The Alchemist, a small apothecary shop also located in downtown Seven Hills.

During the All Hallows' Eve festivities of last year, our town's mayor, Silas VanHoy, was murdered in the town square, and our lives devolved into chaos. Mayor VanHoy had plans to put a Value Mart downtown, wiping out local businesses, which created a lot of animosity between him, myself, my sisters, and other local business owners—including my childhood best friend, Deidra Parker, who also owns a small business downtown, a bakery aptly named Seven Sweets.

After his death, we, along with other business owners, came under suspicion in his murder. Deidra, having gotten into a public screaming match with Mayor VanHoy not 24 hours before his murder didn't help. In a way, my sisters and I were already suspected murderers. Many of the Seven Hills locals believed that my biological father, Jasper Alden, did not disappear, but was murdered by my mother, Diana, and her sister, my Aunt Elaina. Despite the fact that we were not yet adults when this all occurred, it was long rumored that me and my sisters, Theo and Tara, helped them dispose of his body—in our backyard of all places.

But, of course, we hadn't. At least my sisters and I never helped our Mother and Aunt Elaina dispose of the body. Nor did we have any knowledge of what happened to Jasper Alden. We also didn't have any knowledge of what happened to Mayor VanHoy. But after a little amateur sleuthing, I, along with my friend and famed professor, Dr. Ronnie Jackman, found out VanHoy was laundering money with the help of local business owner, Hansen Mills.

The scheme was more complex than we could have ever imagined, as it involved not just VanHoy and Mills, but several locals and a member of the police force as well. "Hometown hero" Cliff Bishop, we later discovered, was the muscle of the money laundering operation, and the local cop involved in the scheme was a friend of ours from childhood, Jimmy Dickson. My sisters and I knew both Cliff Bishop and Jimmy Dickson our entire lives.

Everything came to a head when I walked in on Hansen, Dickson, and Mrs. VanHoy arguing. I had simply wanted to drop off a box of supplies from The Alchemist for the pageant to Mrs. VanHoy, and I was quite shocked to find myself in the scene that I had stumbled upon. I had suspected Hansen Mills of murdering Mayor VanHoy, which caused me to try to get Mrs. VanHoy to leave. Mills, who was very intoxicated at the time, tried to choke me to shut me up.

Thinking about this incident caused me to rub my neck. I was lucky that I was alive. But the true shock came after the incident, when I was safely downtown at the police station. I discovered that Mrs. VanHoy confessed to the crime. She murdered her husband in cold blood in the town square with a blunt object. She confessed to the detective investigating Mr. VanHoy's murder, Detective Mike Harrison, who I haven't seen or heard from since that day. *"The day."*

I checked my phone. Twenty-four voicemails. *Not bad*, I thought. I did get out of bed, but I deleted all the voicemails without listening to them. I had been poked and prodded enough. I participated in numerous interviews at the station already. I told my story, clearly, over and over again. If the police wanted to move forward, they had to do so without me. The process had taken months, and I was done.

They already had everything they needed to charge Mrs. VanHoy. They had everything they needed to charge Hansen, and they would have to figure out the Jimmy Dickson situation for themselves. I did not like the interview process, and sitting on the hard metal chairs made my back ache. I did not like the stale coffee, the faux sympathy, or, worst of all, the questions about my family.

"Since I have you here," the young redheaded officer from *"the day"* began. She transitioned casually, too casually, during one interview. "I thought I'd ask you about a cold case."

My blood turned icy. There could only be one cold case. In my time since *"the day,"* as I lovingly referred to it, I had learned the redheaded woman's name, Stacey. Officer Stacey Jacoby.

"What cold case?" I asked weakly, barely croaking the question out.

Officer Jacoby made a concerted effort to look professional. "Jasper Alden?"

"What about him?" I was also making a concerted effort—a concerted effort not to bolt.

"He was your father," she stated, almost as if she was attempting to jog my memory.

"I know," I responded. My mouth tasted sour. I cleared my throat. "I know who he is."

"Do you know anything about his whereabouts?" she asked, earnestly, inelegantly.

Did she really think she would be the person to solve the case? Did she think that all of this would truly be resolved by asking me this question? Her approach was so pathetic, I almost wanted to laugh. I wanted to laugh, then cry, then scream, all from emotional exhaustion. Instead, I just looked into my Styrofoam cup of coffee as if the answers might be in there if I concentrated hard enough.

"I do not."

"Do you know of Elaina Culpepper's whereabouts?"

I was physically shivering then, "I do not."

Jacoby did not ask of Diana Culpepper's whereabouts as she was buried in Seven Hills Cemetery, cancer taking her years ago.

She leaned back in her chair. Her red hair shining like flames under the florescent light. She hit the button on her pen a few times against her chin. I could tell she was contemplating whether she should proceed. *She would be a horrible poker player*, I thought grimly. After a long silence, she nodded.

"Okay, well, we will give you a call."

I stood up so fast, the metal chair screeched across the floor.

That night, when I came home, I announced that I would no longer be participating in the investigation. Both Theo and Tara were seated in what Mom and Aunt Elaina called "the drawing room" when I burst through the door. Both looked up, acknowledged that they heard me, but neither questioned me. They were probably talking about this and my behavior amongst themselves since the holidays.

"I gotta know though," I burst. "Do you guys think Mom and Aunt Elaina murdered our father? And is the fucker actually buried in our backyard?"

It was the longest of pauses. We had been tiptoeing around this subject for months, since All Hallows' Eve, since *"the day."* *"The day"* that I had been choked, nearly to death, by a drunk and belligerent criminal. *"The day"* that I found out that a person who I trusted, a person that I had cared about, murdered her husband in cold blood in the town's square. *"The day"* that I found out that others in the town, people I had trusted, people I had grown up with, were also "in" on nefarious activity, money laundering and who knows what else.

At this point, why wouldn't I think the people who I'd loved most in this world were also capable of anything—even murder. It was hard to reconcile that my mother and my aunt, the women I knew—beautiful, loving, comforting, even entrancing—could also be something else, could also be murderers. I shuddered.

Theo spoke first, measuring her words carefully. She looked so much like Mom sitting there in her old chair, dark green and wingback. The fire blazed in the fireplace behind her, making her face dark. She picked at the armchair for a moment, adding to what age and wear had already done to the antique. "I think there are ways we can find out. I never told either you this, but I received a call from Aunt Elaina—just once since she left. She told me that anything and everything we need is in the house."

I was taken aback. *Theo heard from Aunt Elaina?* She never mentioned this to us.

"What does that even mean?" I demanded, my voice sounding harsher than I wanted it to.

"Come on, Theo," Tara exclaimed, exacerbated. She looked like she wanted to stand, but just shifted in her seat on the sofa. "She meant we could live here or sell the house or whatever. We have the business and our spot downtown as an asset as well."

"No," Theo shook her head emphatically. "She told me that anything and everything we need to know, the truth about our family, is *hidden* in the house."

"And you never told us?!" I cried, my voice rising.

"I didn't know what it meant exactly. You remember, Treasure, Mom and Aunt Elaina were always speaking in riddles."

"Could Jasper Alden's remains be in the fucking house?!" Tara cried, interrupting Theo, her voice screeching.

"Calm down," Theo said meekly, tears forming in the corner of her eyes.

Tara looked at Theo and then at me. "Whatever, I'm sorry. It's just a lot. I've been looked at as basically an accomplice to murder my entire life, and I was practically a baby when this all happened."

"I know, Tara," I interjected. "If anyone gets it, we do. Theo, can you tell us exactly what Aunt Elaina said?"

"I, of course, do not remember word for word exactly what she said. I was stressed when she left. I had, essentially, two parents, and then I was on my own, and on my own with two young girls. I know we weren't kids, but there was so much to figure out. A business to run... a large estate to maintain... taxes...."

I was disappointed in myself for not stopping to think about the number this had done on Theo. She always seemingly had it all together. She never seemed stressed by all the burdens, annoyed at times, sure, but never stressed. She handled everything with more grace than I could muster for even one day in my life.

"I don't know, it was years ago…" Theo continued, "But it was something to the effect of whatever I needed to know about Jasper… about our family… was here… on the property."

"Oh God!" Tara practically screamed.

My stomach bottomed out. "Okay… okay… I'm sure she didn't mean he was literally buried here. Maybe she just meant if we wanted to know what happened with Jasper…"

"How would they know what happened to Jasper, if they didn't *kill* Jasper?!" Tara howled, her eyes practically bugging out of her head.

"Mom and Aunt Elaina didn't kill Jasper. There's no way they did that. They couldn't. They weren't… like that… I'm sure she just meant that there was paperwork or something in the house…" Theo's voiced trailed off, sounding weak.

"Aunt Elaina meant there was paperwork in the house? Paperwork?! You two are both so messed up. Theo, all you do is cover for everyone, and Treasure, all you do is lay in bed feeling sorry for yourself. I'm outta here," Tara declared, springing up from the sofa.

Theo also leapt to her feet, "Sit down, Tara!" she bellowed. Tara looked aghast. Tara and I exchanged looks, shocked. Tara sat back down. "And all you do is run away, Tara. You know what? I'm sick of both of your shit. I'm sorry I didn't tell you about Aunt Elaina's call. It was a thirty-second call, and forgive me, but I had a lot on my plate at the time," she said sarcastically. She paused, tears welling up in her eyes. "I just… I really don't think Mom and Aunt Elaina would hurt someone…."

"I know," I said, feeling tears spring to my own eyes. "I know."

"Don't you guys just want to know? Once and for all. Just know?" Tara asked, her voice earnest. She was shifting on her feet, her hands gesturing wildly.

"I think I need to know," I answered honestly. "I think I need to know what happened. Whatever the outcome is. We need to close this chapter once and for all."

We looked at Theo, waiting for her response. She took a deep breath. "Let's look around. See what we find. But—" she paused looking at both of us in the eye, "Treasure, you are getting your shit together, and Tara, you are staying put."

Silence was our agreement.

The month was March, and still very cold, but a hopeful cold. Everything was starting to warm up, a promise that spring was, indeed, coming. There was still snow on the ground in some places, but even in those patches of white, green grass poked through. The air smelled like wet earth, as we all hopped in Theo's Chevrolet Caprice Classic station wagon—once our mother's car—and rode to The Alchemist together. We needed all-hands-on-deck to prepare for the Ostara Festival—now just days away. Ostara is a Pagan holiday, celebrating the Spring Equinox. The word Ostara comes from the Goddess Eostre, a female deity symbolizing abundance, fertility, and new beginnings. Ostara couldn't have come at a better time. We were all ready for a new beginning.

The Ostara Festival started out very small in Seven Hills. In fact, The Alchemist probably was the first to publicly recognize the holiday. As a child, it seemed we were the only ones to celebrate, but eventually other businesses caught on. While Ostara was nowhere near as big as All Hallows' Eve or Christmas, it was becoming more popular, and every year, more and more businesses participated.

When I was kid, participating in Ostara, at least in a public capacity, was limited to hanging up endless paper-rabbit decorations and helping Mom and Aunt Elaina whip up all-natural cleaning supplies—so fragrant that one could smell The Alchemist from blocks away.

Now, almost all the businesses in Seven Hills participated in the small festival in the town's square. Like All Hallows' Eve, businesses would set up booths, selling various wares and spring treats. Deidra was the main proprietor of the spring treats. She would whip up chocolate covered marshmallow cookies, homemade strawberry shortcake, angel food cake, and meringue cookies so light they melted in your mouth in seconds. Nothing quite kicks off a new beginning like a sugar high.

Mrs. VanHoy, in years past, would organize a large egg hunt—more related to the commercialism of Easter than to Ostara itself. Hundreds of plastic eggs would be placed all through town, filled with processed sugar of all varieties.

Unlike a traditional Easter egg hunt, the Ostara Hunt often required mittens, and it ended with hot chocolate or coffee, as it was often too early for true spring weather. One year, it was so cold and wet, the egg hunt was moved to the high school gym, where essentially eggs were laid on the gym floor several feet apart, resulting in a very short hunt. I wondered who was organizing the egg hunt now and shuddered, thinking of the fabulous Mrs. VanHoy reduced to sitting in a prison cell somewhere. I never could quite bring myself to ask where she was taken.

The Alchemist was slow this morning, so Theo, Tara, and I had an opportunity to work on the materials for the festival for a couple of hours. We planned on doing a small booth filled with our natural cleaning products, spring-themed candles, sage bundles, all-natural lotions, and bug repellants.

We were all working when the familiar clang of our sleigh bells sounded, signifying someone entered the store, causing all of us to look up. It was Ronnie, holding a teal box, tied with a singular white ribbon, topped with the familiar Seven Sweets logo, and a to-go crate filled with coffee cups. I could smell the coffee from across the room: hazelnut.

"Hey guys!" he greeted with a large smile on his handsome face. "I thought you all might appreciate a mid-morning snack, while we work on the booth."

I smiled, taking note of him. Ronnie was tall, classically good-looking, but in an unassuming way, an oblivious way. He had light brown hair, neatly trimmed above his ears. While he was small and quiet when we were kids, he is quite tall now, with a lean, muscular build.

Ronnie was dressed unusually for him. Normally, he wore some combination of blazer and slacks, but today he was dressed in what looked to be an old light blue tee shirt and dark brown cargo pants. There were paint splatters on his pants already. Tiny specks of a pale yellow. Suddenly, I wondered about where Ronnie lived, his home. *Where did he live? What did it look like in there? What colors had he painted the walls?*

"Work on the booth?" Tara repeated, standing up from where she was bundling sage on a flattened cardboard box on the floor. She placed her hands on her slender hips. "Who invited you?"

"I invited him," Theo said, shooting Tara an annoyed look. "I asked Ronnie if he would like to help paint the hare. I want a giant hare on one side of the booth and a large Easter-looking egg on the other."

"Who's going to paint all this today?" Tara demanded. "Because I have an expensive outfit on." She gestured to her outfit, a matching set of cream-colored fuzzy leggings and a matching cropped sweatshirt. I rolled my eyes. She really was insufferable at times.

"Treasure can help him," Theo sighed.

"Yes, her outfit looks much cheaper than mine," she said flatly, walking over to the box of goodies from Seven Sweets. "Oh! Lemon-blueberry muffins! My favorite!"

She pulled a large muffin from the box and peeled down the wrapper, smelling it before she took a large bite.

"I know," Ronnie said, "I remembered." Ronnie was clearly unfazed by Tara. He gave her a rueful smile before directing his attention to me. "Shall we?" Ronnie asked, turning to me, his eyes fixed on mine. For a moment, I felt slightly off kilter. I hadn't seen him in a while.

"Why not?" I agreed, smiling at him. "I wouldn't want to waste a 'cheap outfit.'" I shot Tara a look, which she ignored.

I hurriedly tidied what I had been working on—drying petals on sheet paper. The petals would be used to make labels and to be crushed and bottled when needed. I also planned on putting petals in my candles during the spring and summer seasons. I wanted vibrant pink, purple, blue, and yellow flowers on every square inch of The Alchemist. The thought gave me a light feeling, an almost hopeful feeling. Spring was coming.

Ronnie and I stepped into the back of The Alchemist, our large supply room, where we assessed the large wooden egg and hare cutouts propped up against our craft shelf. Paul Richards, the owner of The Craft, across and down the street next to Seven Sweets, cut out the large figures for us. We began to gather paint and brushes, debating if we should paint a white or a brown hare and what colors should go on the Easter egg.

"We could do a really cool neon egg," Ronnie suggested, pointing to some neon-colored paints on our craft shelf.

"Not a 'really cool neon egg,'" I laughed, nudging his hip a bit with mine. He laughed, making eye contact with me and then looked away, turning a bit pink.

"Traditional colors, then?" Ronnie asked, his smile bright.

"I can't imagine Theo's reaction to a neon egg. She is a bit of a holiday purist."

"Okay, fine," Ronnie conceded with a bit of faux disappointment in his voice.

After we gathered the supplies needed, we went into the alley behind The Alchemist, where the dumpsters sat, exiting out of the rarely used backdoor. It was a bit wet back there, as snow was still working on melting away, but we were able to find a few dry places to place the large egg and hare cutouts. We were painting for a couple of minutes in silence before one of us spoke.

"So, you didn't have work today?" I asked, working to fill the silence. Very rarely did cars come down this back alley. So, we had the ability to work without much interruption.

"I took today off," he stated matter-of-factly, his eyes fixed on his task. We decided to go with a brown hare.

"Couldn't resist painting the hare, could you?" I teased with a laugh.

"Naw. Plus, I feel like I haven't seen you in forever," Ronnie said, almost sheepishly. "You don't answer my texts."

This was true. Ronnie and I had spent a lot of time together in the fall, almost every day for a while. But when it was all said and done, I simply didn't have the energy. This must be why I didn't have a large circle of friends. I primarily hung out with my sisters and Deidra, on whose friendship I frankly didn't have to do much work to maintain.

"I know," I acknowledged, a ball of guilt forming in my stomach. "I'm sorry about that. It's been a little hard lately to get... I don't know... motivated, I guess."

"You've been through a lot," he said, quietly. His face concentrated on mixing some paint on a small, white, plastic paint palette.

"Yea..." I responded, my voice coming out sounding weaker than I wanted it to. Tears were welling up in my eyes. I could feel everything I had experienced in my body, over the course of my whole life, held there like a vase full of heavy marbles. I needed to get rid of all of it, cleanse it away. I suddenly understood the concept of baptism so clearly. I wanted to get submerged into a pool of water, leave all the heaviness behind, come back someone new, someone lighter. I turned my head, pretending to look down the alley until the tears dried.

"Have you heard anything about what's going on with Jimmy Dickson?" Ronnie asked, tentatively.

"I sort of stopped participating in the investigation stuff. Not that I know anything about Jimmy or what he was involved with anyway," I admitted.

"Yea," he nodded, pausing his progress on the hare to look at me for a second. He returned back to painting. "You remember his mom, Donna Dickson, right? She was one of our lunch ladies in elementary school?" I nodded.

"She goes to the Trinity Church," Ronnie continued. "You know the one downtown? My mom goes there too, has been a member her entire life. I guess Donna and Cliff's mom talk on and on about Jimmy's removal from the force. They serve on some board there together. She has been openly hostile to my mom. Thinks I—and probably all of you—had something to do with him getting 'wrongly terminated.'"

"I'm so sick of this shit," I blurted, causing Ronnie to look up from his task, his paint brush suspended in midair. "I feel like we are blamed for everything. Sorry, lady, but your son was seemingly involved in some shady shit. That has nothing to do with me or my family. You would think that I would hold more grudges. I mean, I was the one who was assaulted, almost killed."

Again, I was transported back to the feeling of Hansen's large hands around my neck, the feeling of panic as my airway was blocked.

"I know," Ronnie agreed solemnly. "I'm so sorry."

Just then, Tara opened the back door. She looked at both of us, a mixture of annoyance and alarm on her pretty face. "There's a problem."

We all convened back in the shop part of The Alchemist, and I noticed that Deidra had arrived. She held her phone up, showing Theo what appeared to be a news article.

"Hey," Deidra stated instead of greeted. "I guess a girl went missing yesterday. Here in Seven Hills. I'm showing Theo the article now."

"Really, oh my gosh!" I exclaimed, looking at Ronnie who also looked concerned. "That's horrible. How old is she?"

"16 or 17, I believe the article said," Deidra responded, looking over Theo's shoulder as she scrolled through her phone. "Her name is Jenna Bishop."

"Bishop," I repeated, dumbly. My mind whirled. I knew the name, but, for the life of me, could not place it. Connect the dots. *Bishop. Bishop.*

"Apparently, her car was found on State Route 2," Theo relayed. "Near our home."

Theo stopped reading and turned to look at Deidra, the cellphone still suspended in her hand, and then at all of us. A look of horror crossed her face. I could feel my heart rate increase. *Bishop. Bishop. Bishop*, I repeated internally, like a chant. Then, it hit me. *Bishop.*

"Bishop? Like Cliff Bishop?" I queried everyone and no one in particular.

"I... I don't know..." Deidra stammered. "There could be a connection..."

"Okay, so let me get this straight. A girl is missing with the last name Bishop, as in Cliff Bishop, and her car was found disabled near our property—at least as far as we can tell from the information in the article you're reading?"

"Oh, fuck me!" Tara exclaimed, exasperated.

The rest of the day went by slowly. Ronnie and I finished our painting of the giant egg and hare with no incident, occasionally refreshing our phones to check for news of the missing girl, Jenna Bishop, a name I now had committed to memory. Ronnie hugged me tight before he left.

"Promise me you won't be a stranger," he said, his chin resting on my head still in a full embrace.

"I won't," I promised and wondered if I was telling the truth.

My sisters and I put everything away for the day, counted the money in the register, and turned the sign in the door from Open to Closed. We should have been incredibly happy after all we accomplished today, but there was a sense of unease. Tara checked her phone again.

"No news?" Theo asked.

"Nothing new," Tara responded, shoving her phone into her handbag that sat perched on the counter next to the register.

"Alright, let's go home."

We traveled most of the way home in relative silence. The silence was only broken occasionally for contemplation over what to have for dinner. Eventually, we all decided to just eat whatever we could find. I planned on indulging in a nice big bowl of sugary cereal in the privacy of my room.

I started a fire in the fireplace in my bedroom quarters, my cereal seated on the mantle of the fireplace. I warmed my hands and then grabbed my bowl, eating in the most unladylike way, milk dribbling down my chin. A new year and yet, it was already a hard year. I felt my mind was a mental cage that I desperately wanted to escape from. I did not want to live this way anymore.

"Okay," I said aloud to myself, abandoning my bowl of cereal on the rug where I had been previously seated. "Enough."

I walked over to my makeshift bookshelf, made from the original kitchen cabinets installed in Culpepper Manor, and grabbed my tarot cards and journal, my book of shadows. I usually pulled a card for the start of the new year, a card that would signify what was to come. It seemed fitting that this year, I was only getting around to the task in March. I flipped through my book of shadows to last year's entry. I took a few minutes to find the day that I pulled my card for the year.

According to my entry, I pulled The Wheel of Fortune card, signifying that events would take place that would impact my fate. I sat back on the rug, leaning against my small couch, briefly dropping my head onto a cushion, and stretched my legs to warm my feet by the fire. The Wheel of Fortune card felt eerily accurate. The events of last year, events that I had no control over, had impacted my life greatly—maybe even more than I realized now.

I stood, grabbed some incense from a wooden box on one of my shelves, and lit it in my sitting room. I circled my quarters with the stick, concentrating on the corners and in my closet, moving to my bedroom area, opening a window for the energy to escape. I wanted a clear space before I picked a card. I swiped the stick over my tarot deck a few times, concentrating on what my new year would look like. After setting the incense in my holder, a handmade incense holder painted with moons and stars, I shuffled my deck. Moment of truth. *What would this year hold?*

I stopped shuffling and pulled a card from the deck, the energy so electric I could feel it tingling up my arm. I turned the card over. The Magician card stared back at me. *The Magician.* My breath caught. The Magician was an almost sacred card that signified creation, control over one's circumstances, and the ability to use energy to change and transform one's life. Power. Magick.

How could The Magician possibly be my card for the year? I couldn't even magically extricate myself from my bed unless I absolutely had to. I jotted down the card in my book of shadows and let the incense continue to burn as I brushed my teeth in my en-suite bathroom. I would take my cereal bowl down to the kitchen tomorrow. I entered my sleeping area and crawled into bed, cocooning myself in a thick layer of blankets. I had felt fatigued all day, but suddenly now, I felt a bit energized. *The Magician. But how was that even possible?*

I got up and out of bed. I walked out onto my balcony, sliding the doors open and shut behind me. I stared out into the trees, the bare branches and needles swaying in the moonlight, and it dawned on me. I could be The Magician. I could create my life in any way that I wanted.

I closed my eyes, and my thoughts drifted to Detective Harrison. The memory of his face was blurred a little, but I could remember his energy clearly: masculine, powerful, even sensual. He once accused me of being a sort of magician, accused me of frightening Hansen Mills, even though he was the one who assaulted me—choked me. I think his words were, "scared the living daylights out of him."

To my knowledge, I had done nothing to Mills. Perhaps Mills made up the story to convince law enforcement that he had felt a real threat, had a reason to put his meaty, red hands about my neck and squeeze. Or maybe I did have Magick qualities. Qualities lying dormant. My mother did. My Aunt Elaina did. Or at least in my childhood mind and memories they did. I closed my eyes then and envisioned my mom and my aunt. I tried to dig deeper into my subconscious and envision my ancestors. A sort of meditation.

Detective Harrison came crashing through my mind again. I tried to remember the sound of his voice, remember how his blue eyes would fix on me. I wondered where he was and if he was coming back. He relayed to me on *"the day"* that he would be staying for a while. Yet, he was gone. Kristy Pickles, the town gossip, had reported as much to me. Said he ran off with some girl to Boston, nodding smugly as she told me.

"Poor Lydia," Kristy had said, shaking her head, laying a hand over her heart theatrically, "she must be heartbroken."

Lydia Swinger was a girl from our high school class. Allegedly, she was seen with Harrison multiple times. I wondered if this was true. I wondered if anything I heard about Harrison from Kristy was true. I shivered.

Standing out on my balcony was too cold this late at night, wearing just an oversized Backstreet Boys sweatshirt, pajama pants, and fuzzy socks. I entered back into my room, shutting the door behind me. The warmth of the fire, filling the space, welcomed me back. I slid back into my bedroom, under my flannel comforter. *The Magician*, I thought. The Magician. The room smelled of fire, incense, our laundry detergent, and vaguely of lavender and sage, how my mother always smelled. I closed my eyes.

I awoke to a sound, causing me to sit up in bed. Sleepily, I slid out from my comforter and padded my way into my sitting room. It was pitch black, only a few embers burning in the fireplace, casting a slight orangey glow to the room.

The room felt incredibly cold, despite the fire still struggling to hang on. I scanned the room for the cause of the noise when suddenly, I had an awareness that someone sat in my chair near the fireplace. My whole body snapped to attention. I was wide awake then, gripping the French doors separating the rooms, alarmed, blinking my eyes, straining to see in the darkness.

A shadow, a figure. I could see the outline of a face, a profile, staring into the embers. Male. I blinked once and blinked again, my heart pounding through my chest, pounding in my ears, filling the silence. Goosebumps formed on my arms, my legs, standing so stark my appendages throbbed. I blinked again, and the figure was gone. I rubbed my eyes. No one. No one was there. Just the wingback chair. But someone had been there. Sitting there. I felt sick to my stomach, but whatever it was—whoever he was—he was gone.

"Gone," I whispered, wondering if I should pinch myself. Was this a night terror? Didn't people dream they were awake, when asleep? Or did that only happen in the movies?

I flipped on the lights, feeling calmer. Suddenly I noticed the smell or, more accurately, smells. My room now smelled like mildew, water, rot—smells that should not be here, especially after a night of lighting incense and hours of a fire burning.

I examined the chair, and then walked slowly towards it, as if it was a rabid dog, liable to spook and bite. The chair was, indeed, empty. I touched the seat. Empty. My eyes drifted down below the chair. There, beneath the chair, was a small puddle of water.

"What in the world?" I said, out loud, placing my fingers in the puddle.

I touched the chair again. Dry. I stood on the chair. Ceiling: dry. I had no animals in my room. At least, I didn't think so. I sat on the edge of my small couch, staring at the chair, until finally retreating to my bed. I scrolled on my phone for an hour before grabbing a pillow and crawling into Tara's bed with her.

"Something weird happened," I whispered, as I slipped in under the covers.

"What's new," she croaked, sleepily, and rolled over.

The next thing I knew, it was morning.

Chapter 2

I was getting dressed for the day when my phone chirped with a news alert—yet another notice about Jenna's disappearance. I glanced at my phone, seeing the article entitled, "Local Girl Missing in Seven Hills" on my lock screen before I finished pulling my sweatshirt over my head. I unlocked my phone and opened the article. I skimmed through the first couple of paragraphs, passing the information we already knew: Jenna Bishop, age 16, vehicle had been found yesterday, abandoned on State Route 2.

I scrolled through the news article, but there were very few new details. It appeared that Jenna, for reasons unknown, pulled over to the side of the road. What happened next was also not yet known—or at least not yet shared with the public. Thankfully, according to all the articles I had read thus far, there wasn't any evidence to suggest that Jenna had been hurt—at least not in the vehicle. This was hopeful. Maybe, she would be found—and found alive. I scrolled down.

There were over one hundred comments on the article already. Some speculated that Jenna had probably left the vehicle, seeking help and was hurt in the woods; others speculated that Jenna had been kidnapped, the perpetrator abandoning the vehicle where it was found. One person even pointed out that Jenna's car was found near our property. My heart picked up the pace as I read a comment from User117.

User117: Things that make you go hmmmm… another missing person linked to the Culpepper property.

The comment had two replies under it.

CatMom2010: I'm not surprised.

User117: No one who is from here would be.

I gaped at the comments, the urge to defend myself and my family so visceral, it overtook my entire body. I clicked on User117. No profile picture. No profile. A burner account. An account created to make this comment. I felt ill. I did the same investigation with CatMom2010, and again, nothing. I took a deep breath, already feeling a familiar tightness in my chest. The next urge, to close the curtains and get back in bed, hit me in a wave. I remembered Theo's words, her suggestion I get my shit together, and sighed. I locked my phone, grabbed my purse, and darted down the hallway and the back staircase to the kitchen before I could change my mind.

Theo was already awake, stirring a pot with one hand, scrolling through her phone with the other. She was dressed in a pair of sensible slacks and a button-down shirt, apron on top. Her black hair was wound into a topknot, little strands coming out and curling from the steam of the pot. She looked just like Mom: black hair, bright green eyes, a prominent nose, and high cheekbones. A classically beautiful face, each angle complementing the next perfectly.

"Did you see this?" she asked, not even raising her eyes from her phone.

"Yes," I stated, joining her at the stove. I wondered if she meant the article itself or the comments below. I tentatively asked, "What do you think happened to Jenna?"

"I don't know," Theo responded, shaking her head. "I can't even imagine the pain her family is in right now." Theo paused and looked at me as if she was rethinking her last statement. We didn't really know our family member who went missing, but we still knew pain from someone missing. I rubbed her arm, choosing not to bring up the comments below the article. We already knew people would suspect us, so why did it matter?

Instead, I just whispered, "I know."

Tara joined us in the kitchen, dressed in a camel-colored sweater and a pair of faded blue jeans. Her dirty-blonde hair was also tied into a topknot—the Culpepper signature look. Tara looked much less like Mom, and by extension, Theo. Although Tara was quite thin, her face was rounder than Mom and Theo's, her features softer, her eyes blue.

We sat around the center island, eating the steel-cut oats that Theo had been prepping on the stove with some dried cranberries, sliced almonds, and a little pure maple syrup for some extra sweetness. What would normally be a delicious breakfast felt heavy on my spoon and tongue. Each bite felt like cement landing on the brick that had formed in my stomach. As we sat, we continued reading news articles and social media about Jenna's disappearance.

"The Sheriff's Office is requesting volunteers to help with the search," Theo shared. "Looks like they will be searching close to where her vehicle was found. I think we should help. It's right up the road. The search may even extend onto our property."

My mind flashed to User117. This, of course, as we knew it would be, was part of the problem. I took another labored bite of my steel-cut oats and looked over at Tara, who was nodding.

"There's a number to call for details. I'll do that now," Theo continued, leaving her seat and walking out of the kitchen, most likely going to the study or even the foyer to make the call.

"Trinity Church is having a prayer vigil this evening," Tara shared. "Jenna was a member. Part of their youth group and choir. Seemed pretty involved."

I made a noise that I hoped sounded like an acknowledgement as I stared into my breakfast.

"Do we know if Jenna was related to Cliff?" I asked nervously, stirring the contents of my bowl. "I mean, they must be, right? This is such a small area. I'm sure they are—at least—distantly related."

"Yes...." Tara's voice trailed off, and she flipped through her phone. "I just saw something about that... cousins!" she suddenly exclaimed. "They're cousins. Poor girl! Goes missing and has Cliff for a cousin. Damn."

I gave Tara a stern look.

"What?" She shrugged her shoulders. "The girl can't catch a break!"

Tara paused and looked at me. Her face shifted into someone a little more serious. "Are you going to tell me what happened last night?" I stared back at her, not sure where to begin. Thankfully, Theo reentered the kitchen before I could answer. Tara redirected her attention.

"We can join the search group up the road. There should be a tent for us to check in."

"When can we go?" I asked, a sense of dread forming in the pit of my stomach.

"We can go now," Theo explained, dropping her dishes into the sink. "They want to get started right away."

Tara and I stood, almost in unison, and did the same. I paused when Tara walked away, watching the leftover, steel-cut oats slide from my bowl and into the sink.

Theo drove us to the search location in our mother's old Chevrolet Caprice Classic station wagon. The day was overcast, the sun barely peeking through the thick layer of clouds, as cold and gloomy outside as I felt inside. The ground was largely devoid of snow, but little mounds of snow still lined the highway, dark, almost black, with mud and rock.

We pulled into a little corn field, or what would be a cornfield in the late summer and fall, across the highway from where Jenna's vehicle was found—only about a mile away from Culpepper Manor. We exited the vehicle and joined the small crowd that was forming around a white pop-up tent. There looked to be about fifty to sixty, mostly middle-aged or older, people present, all talking at once; a small beehive working to find a member of the colony.

"Alright, alright," a mustached sheriff's deputy hollered, attempting to quiet the crowd. He was an older man with a rounded belly, his uniform slightly askew. "Everyone, listen up. I only want to say this once. The more time wasted here is less time we're looking for Jenna. I'm Deputy Terrance from the Hanigan County Sheriff's Department. Everyone needs to check in at this table before you leave the area." He pointed towards a folding card table where another deputy, so classically handsome he was almost nondescript, was sitting.

"Get a reflective vest, get assigned a search area and team. Pick up a couple of flags." There were some mumbles from the crowd. "If you see something, you plant a flag near it, you tell your team leader, and you call it in over the radio. You don't touch it! You got that? Don't touch anything. Just call it in and we'll determine if its relevant." He took a deep breath, audible in the microphone.

"And, call Jenna's name as you're searching, but remember to give her time to respond. She may be injured, stuck somewhere, and if everyone is yelling at the same time, we won't be able to hear her respond." There seemed to be murmurs of agreement. Some in the crowd nodded in acknowledgement.

"Okay then," the deputy continued, adjusting his gun belt, "we're going to break into small groups; we'll give you a map and an assignment when you sign-in."

I spotted Brent Silverton in the crowd, a man we went to school with, dressed in a puffy winter jacket, a stocking hat pulled low on his forehead, covering his dark hair, his ruddy cheeks peeking out below. My mind flashed to a scene at The Witches Brew last year. My sisters, Deidra, and I taking shots with Brent, Cliff joining us at some point, the feeling of getting drunker and drunker as the night went on and—Detective Harrison. I had spotted his shiny black hair in the crowd. Although the memory is blurry, I remember walking down a long, dark hallway to the bathroom, music blaring, talking to Detective Harrison, leaning on him. Or maybe just wanting to lean on him. I can't remember which.

I gave Brent a slight nod of acknowledgement, prompting him to elbow the large man standing next to him, turned with his back towards us. The man turned and looked at me and my sisters. It was Cliff Bishop.

"Oh, hell no!" Cliff roared, coming towards us. "There is no way the three of you are getting involved in this search! Her car was found close to your property!"

I grabbed onto Theo's arm and took a step back. Tara, however, took a step forward.

"We're here to help, Cliff!" Tara yelled back. "Why can't we help with the search?"

"Because you three probably had something to do with her disappearance!"

"What?!" Theo and Tara responded, shocked by Cliff's outburst. I wasn't shocked. User117 and CatMom2010 popped into my head. Of course, there would be people who thought we were involved in Jenna's disappearance. There were people who thought we were involved in our father's disappearance and presumed murder. There were people, last year, who assumed we were involved in Mayor VanHoy's murder; maybe some that still assumed we were involved, even though Mrs. VanHoy had confessed. Theo and Tara knew this, but perhaps, the shock came from someone laying this out so plainly. Confronting us, in public, when we were least expecting it. A throwback to a time long ago, a time of less civility. Point your finger and shout, "Witch!" Then, watch and see what happens.

The crowd in the tent was now looking at us. Buzzing again. One homogenous hive that could turn on us at any second. Attack. The nest had been poked. I struggled to find something to say, anything. I should shout. Beat my chest in upset, but I said nothing, feeling the familiar paralysis I often did when confronted with something uncomfortable. A trauma response, I knew, and yet had little energy to actually try to resolve. *Why work to improve when you can lay in bed?*

"She's probably on your land somewhere! Hell, she might even be locked in your house!" Cliff was now just a few feet from us, his muscular presence ominous. I heard Deputy Terrance, who was running the meeting, attempt to catch Cliff's attention to no avail. Brent Silverton took a step forward.

"I think you girls should leave," he stated, his gloved hands balled into fists. "We don't need you." So, he believed we might have something to do with this too. There was grumbling agreement from some assembled.

"I can't believe this!" I responded, finally finding my voice. "A young girl is missing! We're here to help! Why on earth would you want us to leave?!"

"Yes, her car was found close to our property," Theo added. "All the more reason for us to be here! We know that land better than anyone!" The group appeared to be growing more agitated. The deputy leading the meeting had clearly lost control.

"I want you out of here!" Cliff screamed, taking another step forward. "If you don't leave right now, so help me, I'll—"

"You'll what?" I heard a familiar voice interrupt Cliff. A firm, commanding voice. One that was unexpected in the current environment. I turned around to see Travis Hodge, someone we had known since grade school, standing behind us. Travis was a Seven Hills police officer and had been at Seven Sweets the morning we found out that Mr. VanHoy had been murdered. Travis had also been partnered with Jimmy Dickson prior to his removal from the force, the man whose mother, Donna Dickson, had decided he was wrongly terminated because of us, at least according to Ronnie. And here Travis was, defending us.

"You'll what?" Travis asked again, coolly placing himself between Cliff, me, and my sisters. Cliff stuttered. He too seemed somewhat surprised by Travis' behavior. Not that Travis was a pushover, but it's not like Travis ever stood up to Cliff while we were in school. *But I guess we're no longer in school*, I thought to myself. Travis' expression was stern as he waited for Cliff's response. When it didn't come, Travis took a step closer to Cliff.

"I don't think you're in any kind of position to be giving orders, Mr. Bishop. May I remind you that your relationship with the Seven Hills Police Department is tenuous, at best? And if it were up to me, you're the one who wouldn't be here." Cliff's face reddened. Cliff looked to Brent for some support, but he had faded into the larger group.

"We are here this morning for Jenna," Travis said to everyone. "If you're not here to help find her, you can go." There were some murmurs amongst the group. The sheriff's deputy who had originally been addressing the group piped back up.

"Attention everyone! If you could please line up single file at the table, we'll get you signed in." Members of the group began shuffling towards the table. I let out a breath that I didn't even know I had been holding. Travis turned and looked at the three of us.

"I'm sorry about that. I have a spot for you. This is a large area, an area that you're familiar with, and we need the bodies. I'm not turning away good help. We're thinking that Jenna walked from her car. The evidence doesn't suggest anything different right now, so it's possible that she walked onto your property. So, we may need access to your land."

"Absolutely, anything that you need," Theo quickly responded. Travis nodded.

"I appreciate your cooperation on this," he stated. He looked at the three of us again.

"You okay with a hike in the woods?" he asked.

"Yes," we all responded in unison.

"Good," Travis affirmed. "Let's get you registered. You can come with me and the Hanigan County Search and Rescue Team. We're going to follow Monte Creek in both directions." Monte Creek was fairly far off of the road. This would have been quite a bit of walking in the dark for a young girl who was unfamiliar with the area.

"Monte Creek?" I questioned.

"We have to cast a wide net. It's very possible that Jenna was not under her own control," Travis explained. "So, we must consider multiple options at this time. It's possible that she was suicidal, was running away, was on drugs, was taken by someone…. Any number of things. At this time, we don't have evidence that she was taken, but we don't have a lot of information about her final hours before she went missing. Everything is on the table."

Travis took us to the registration table to get signed in. We were issued walkie-talkies, reflective vests, and a map of our search area. We then, along with Travis, joined members of Hanigan County Search and Rescue on a trail into the woods.

This trail was known to me and my sisters. We could probably walk it in the dark. Especially as teenagers, we'd follow this trail to get away for a little bit, usually walking it until we got to Monte Creek before turning back. The walk was always so peaceful. A time for reflection. Listening to the sounds of nature made it impossible to dwell on the hundreds of other thoughts rushing through my head at the time. This walk, however, wasn't as peaceful. Although there were moments of quiet, between calls for Jenna, the reason for the trip held in the air. An invisible eeriness, as we all moved beneath the gray sky.

My sisters and I walked with the Hanigan County Search and Rescue Team for the rest of the morning, slowly making our way up both sides of Monte Creek, eyes fixed to the ground, looking for any possible sign of Jenna Bishop. Around noon, we all took a couple of minutes by the side of the creek for some water and granola bars. Theo, Tara, and I sat quietly by the side of the creek, mindlessly watching the water navigate through the polished river rocks.

I dipped my fingers into the icy cold water, recalling the events of the night before. The puddle beneath my chair. The apparition. *Did I dream the whole thing? Imagine it maybe? Maybe I was so freaked out by Jenna's disappearance I had a night terror. Or was someone there, and if so, what did they want?* We long believed that spirits inhabited Culpepper Manor. There were certainly times when guests—when Mom and Aunt Elaina used to have them—would become spooked, mention seeing a strange shadow, or relay feeling a cool breeze where there should be none. These stories were told again and again. But, never had I heard a story of a dripping ghost that smelled of mildew and rot, and this presence seemed different than the others that had been described—darker somehow. Not evil but... troubled maybe.

Travis was farther down the river conferring with one of the members of the search and rescue team. Most times, when we've encountered him on duty, he was in his regular patrol uniform. Today, he was wearing black cargo pants, a thick black sweatshirt, and an external tactical vest that had "Police" in big yellow letters on the back. With his side holster and ballcap, he looked more like a park ranger than a police officer. Travis left the team members and joined us at the side of the creek.

"Well, what's going on?" Tara asked Travis, when he wandered over to where we were taking a break.

"We need to keep following the creek for as far as we can until dusk. At that point, we'll need to head back to the check-in site. The sheriff's office doesn't want any volunteer searchers out in the dark."

"Okay, thank you," Tara responded on behalf of all of us.

"And any news...?" Theo inquired, her voice trailing off.

"And there's no new information about Jenna," Travis added. "If that's what you are asking."

"Damn it," Tara sputtered, looking up into the gray sky.

Theo broke the awkward silence that followed.

"You know, Travis? That was a good thing that you did earlier this morning. Standing up to Cliff. Thank you." Theo looked intently at Travis; her eyes filled with gratitude. Her voice was deep and sincere.

"Especially with everything going on right now," Theo continued, "I know speaking up can't be easy."

"You know what," Travis said, rubbing his chin with his left hand, "it was easy. It is easy. That's what I've realized over these last several months. You know... I knew something was going on with Jimmy." Travis paused and looked at the ground. We all waited breathlessly for what he was about to say next. He took a deep breath. "I mean, I didn't know exactly, but I knew something wasn't right. Too many corners were being cut. Too many procedures weren't being followed. Random sidebars with Cliff at the station. This isn't why I got into law enforcement."

Travis looked up at the three of us. "I feel like an idiot. I didn't know what he was doing. I worked with that man every day. I knew him my entire life, and I didn't know what he was doing right under my nose."

"You can't blame yourself for that, Travis," Theo contested. "You knew him. You trusted him."

"Yeah, but that's not really good enough, is it?" Travis muttered, mostly to himself.

"I wanted to help people," Travis continued. "Give back to the community that I grew up in. I feel like a lot of times I was afraid to speak up. Didn't trust my instincts. Didn't want to rock the boat. Not anymore," he said, shaking his head. "I'm going to call it like I see it," he declared, almost like a reminder to himself. "This thing about blaming your family for every bad thing that happens is bullshit. I'm sorry, but it's a convenient, easy target. It distracts attention from where it should be. I'm going to be better," he said, taking a moment to look each of us in the eyes. "I promise."

You could have knocked me over with a feather. I turned to Tara, who in a rare moment in her life, was rendered absolutely speechless, her mouth slightly opened, seemingly frozen in preparation for a rebuttal that was not needed. Theo, who had been nodding her head while Travis was speaking, got up from the grass and took a couple of steps towards Travis.

"Thank you, Travis. I appreciate—we all appreciate—you... saying that."

Travis nodded and looked briefly at each of us. When none of us spoke, he half-smiled, and walked towards the rest of the search and rescue team, leaving the rest of us quite perplexed on the bank of the creek. I looked at Theo.

"What was that?" I asked. Theo smiled.

"I don't know, but I think that he may be someone else we can count on. Someone other than just Chief Dodd. Jimmy was his partner, but he hasn't said anything to any of us about ruining Jimmy's life."

I thought for a moment. Theo was right: in all the conversations and rumors after Jimmy's arrest, Travis had never said anything to us about the case. Nothing threatening. Nothing in anger. In fact, no one else surrounding the case had told us that Travis was angry at us. Tara played with a few blades of grass between her fingers. I watched her for a moment, wondering if she was going to comment on Travis, his declaration, but she remained silent. I knew Tara wouldn't trust so easily. A few moments later, we began the search again.

The sun began to set, and there was still no sign of Jenna. After the dismissal of the volunteers at dusk, we reluctantly returned to the location of Theo's vehicle, inhaling the familiar scents of lavender and sage as we entered. Theo always kept a sachet filled with the herbs, our mother's scent, beneath the front seat. A small comfort that I was grateful for now, as Theo drove us back to Culpepper Manor.

No one spoke as the gravity of the situation seemed to take up all the space. After we returned home, we quickly changed into a fresh set of clothes and returned to the station wagon. We had decided to meet Deidra and Ronnie at Seven Sweets for a quick dinner, then travel as a group to the vigil at Trinity Church.

"Any news?" Deidra asked tentatively, as we entered the bakery. We were immediately surrounded with the sweet smells of Seven Sweets, followed closely by the rich aroma of Deidra's famous potato soup and some fresh baked yeast rolls. Deidra had closed Seven Sweets up early and set a nice table for us towards the back of the bakery. Ronnie appeared from the back kitchen door, holding a basket of rolls.

"Hi," he greeted, looking between Theo, Tara, and me. "Any sign of Jenna?"

"No. No news, and no sign of Jenna," Theo answered quickly.

Both Deidra and Ronnie exchanged glances and then lowered their gaze in disappointment. They were likely hoping for good news when we arrived.

"Did you help make the rolls?" I asked Ronnie, trying to lighten the mood a bit.

He turned to me and smiled broadly. "No, but I did help carry them out. That counts for something, right?"

I laughed, and Tara, almost audibly, rolled her eyes.

"Well, this is terrible," Deidra declared, ignoring my and Ronnie's side conversation, as she placed some salt and pepper on the table. "What are we supposed to do?"

"Everything we are doing," Ronnie offered, as he rolled up his sleeves. He was dressed in teaching attire, probably having come here straight from the university. "Volunteering as part of the search party, attending the vigil tonight. All these things matter."

"Do they?" Tara demanded flatly. "Because it really felt like we weren't doing anything at all. Walking around the woods all day and no one found a damn thing. Not even a random shoe print. What are 'thoughts and prayers' going to do? Attending a vigil isn't going to bring Jenna home."

"But it tells the family that you support them," Theo quickly countered. "That's worth something."

"Yeah, okay," Tara snorted and rolled her eyes. Deidra, seated now, wordlessly passed the soup and rolls around the table. Tara continued to scroll through her phone, forcing Theo and me to pass the rolls around her, a look of annoyance clearly forming across her face.

"What's wrong?" Theo inquired.

"Have any of you looked at the comments under any of the articles about Jenna's disappearance? People are going crazy. There are actually some people saying that Jenna's disappearance is the result of the 'Seven Hills collective worship of Satan.' Look," she said, handing me the phone. I scrolled through some of the comments.

ORourkeRealty: I knew all of this Satan business would catch up to us eventually.

NanaJane74: Only Jesus can save us!

Andreanelson837: This whole town is possessed! I think the girl was taken!

"Wow," I muttered. I gave Tara her phone back, unwilling to read more. I sighed deeply. At least no one accused us yet under this article, at least in the comments I read.

"Folks like this are opportunistic," Ronnie shrugged. "Tragedy like this, a missing girl who's active in her local church, fear, a seemingly community-wide comfortability with the occult or Witchcraft... it's a recipe for spiritual manipulation. And unfortunately, this type of spiritual manipulation is still common and dangerous. Just like the kind in 1693, when those five women were hanged right here in Seven Hills. This is just the modern form."

"I think the people of Seven Hills know better than that," Deidra said, somewhat confidently. She slurped some of her soup and then added, "Right?" She looked at each of us, whatever confidence she had when making the prior statement quickly evaporating.

"No, Deidra," Tara responded, shaking her head, still scrolling through her phone, ignoring the meal. "Trust me, they don't."

After a depressing dinner, we traveled to Trinity Church, located next to the Seven Hills Town Hall government building that held Ronnie's office downtown, to participate in the candlelight vigil. There was quite a large crowd gathered around the front of the historic church. I was not sure the year the church began, but the brick structure was old, maybe more than one hundred years old, and was often a place of interest for the many tourists that came into town. The building was tall, with a large steeple, a giant clock in the center. A cross sat on the very top of the building, so high in the air, you could see it from The Alchemist. The front lawn of the church was quite large and neatly manicured, fenced in with an old, rusted, black iron gate. All in attendance stood on the lawn, ruining what otherwise would be considered perfect grass. As we moved through the crowd, I noticed volunteers were distributing candles as the light passed through the crowd.

"Stand tall, girls," Theo said quietly, and my body went alert. *Stand tall, girls*, was something that our mother would say when we encountered social situations in which the Culpeppers weren't exactly welcomed. Our mother's expectation was that we always carried ourselves with dignity and kindness, despite the stares and whispered voices. *Stand tall,* she would command. *You have no reason to cower and every reason to be in this space.*

Immediately, the environment hit me: the voices in the crowd had noticeably quieted around us, and multiple people were looking. They were clearly looking between us and someone else walking in our direction with candles: Jimmy Dickson's mother, Donna.

Donna Dickson was older now than the last time I saw her, of course, but I could still tell without a doubt it was her. She wore her long brown hair down in the same dated 90s hairstyle—outdated even when I was a kid, now streaked with gray, complete with the bangs curled up. She was dressed in a pair of dark jeans and a black puffer jacket, unzipped to reveal a multi-colored chunky sweater, another throwback from the 90s. I watched her make a beeline towards us, and I braced for impact. Before Donna could reach us, Chief Dodd, dressed in his police uniform, completely unaware that a scene was about to unfold, walked up and stood beside Tara.

"Good evening, ladies," he said with the proper amount of solemness. "Dr. Jackman," he continued, nodding towards Ronnie. Chief Dodd just stood there, a physical shield with his wide, muscular frame, and nothing more was said as Donna approached our group. Instead of sharing candles with us, she distributed them to everyone else in our area, including Chief Dodd. I heard Tara suck back air in a snort.

"You'll have to excuse me," Chief Dodd said quietly, seemingly noting Donna's strange behavior and Tara's reaction to it. "I will be one of the speakers this evening."

He quietly made his way to the front of the crowd, joining the local pastor and Jenna's family, atop a makeshift stage, complete with a podium and multiple microphones. I watched him as he moved. Chief Dodd, the Seven Hills Chief of Police, was still handsome. He had a friendly face, dimples, and sandy hair, littered with more and more gray as the years went on. His body was as thick as a tree, but all muscle. He probably spent his weekends doing CrossFit or hitting the gym with colleagues.

I remember finding Chief Dodd shooting hoops with a group of teenagers at Seven Hills High School one summer when Deidra and I swore we were "walking off the pounds." He had called my name and waved to me. Deidra and I waved back and then stopped to watch for a few moments. Chief Dodd, at least for the bit we watched, looked like he was somewhat able to keep up with the kids. None of the kids belonged to him. As long as I have known him, Chief Dodd remained childless and unmarried. My family, mainly my mother and Aunt Elaina, had always considered him to be a good man. He was a trusted friend in an organization in which we were otherwise friendless: the police force.

While I was deep in thought, Ronnie had procured some candles from another volunteer and distributed them among our group. We all watched as Chief Dodd stepped up to the microphone and adjusted the black tie that hung from his uniform. He cleared his throat.

"Good evening, ladies and gentlemen. It is with a heavy heart that I address all of you this evening. As you are all aware, sixteen-year-old Jenna Bishop went missing yesterday evening. She was last seen on State Route 2 by the side of her vehicle, approximately five miles out of town. She never made it home. Representatives from the Hanigan County Sheriff's Department, their search and rescue team, and dozens of local volunteers began searching the area in which Jenna's vehicle was located. The search will continue at dawn tomorrow in the same area. If you would like to assist with the search, please see Chief Deputy Talbott here to my right to get signed up." Chief Dodd motioned to his right as the Chief Deputy raised his hand.

"If anyone has any information about Jenna's whereabouts, please contact the sheriff's office." Chief Dodd paused and slowly surveyed the crowd, "Any information, no matter how insignificant, is helpful. You may just have that missing piece that helps to bring Jenna home."

I wondered at this statement. He made it all sound so unbelievably simple.

The rest of the vigil was led by Trinity's Senior Pastor, Grayson Thomas, and included calls for prayers and several hymns. Pastor Thomas made a final appeal for vigilance as the search continued for Jenna before turning over the vigil to Jenna's parents.

Jenna's parents stepped to the front from the crowd, both still holding candles before handing them over to another person I did not recognize on stage. Both of Jenna's parents were young—probably in their early forties. They held on to each other, as if every step was labored, as they approached the microphone together.

"I'm David Bishop and this is my wife, Kristen," the man said into the microphone. I scanned the man for any resemblance to Cliff and found none. David Bishop was tall and lean with an angular face and dark hair. Cliff was boxy, muscular, with light hair, and a square jaw. Of course, however, I knew that uncles and nephews did not always resemble one another. Hell, Tara did not even look that much like Theo, our mother, or me.

David continued, "My wife and I first want to thank all of you for coming out tonight. It is good for us to see so many in our community come out in support of Jenna—our beloved daughter. My wife and I have experienced so much over the course of the last day—confusion, sadness, and even anger—"

Jenna's mother, Kristen, leaned into the microphone, defiantly. "'Do not be deceived, my beloved brethren!' The Lord tells us that 'when lust has conceived, it gives birth to sin; and when sin is accomplished, it brings forth death. Do not be deceived, my beloved brethren!' This time in which we live, this community, has become overrun with the influence of Satan!"

As if in slow motion, Ronnie, Deidra, Theo, Tara, and I all turned to look at each other with raised eyebrows, visible in the candlelight.

Kristen's voice sounded again, loudly, but as if being strangled, she bellowed, "This town has decided that reverence for witches is more important than reverence for our Heavenly Father! Seven Hills openly celebrates the occult! Seven Hills' local economy is built on occult worship! These festivals, these businesses are not simply fun, playful, harmless endeavors! They welcome evil onto your doorstep and the community suffers the consequences! 'Be of sober spirit, be on the alert. Your adversary, the Devil, prowls around like a roaring lion, seeking someone to devour.' That someone is our Father's lovingly devoted daughter, my daughter, our daughter, our sister in Christ, Jenna Bishop!"

Again, we all turned to each other, stunned. This was not the direction any of us expected this night to take. I scanned the crowd. Many in attendance looked stunned as well. Some made eye contact with others in the crowd and shrugged, perhaps chalking up what appeared to be an outburst to the stress of a missing daughter.

Kristen spoke again into the microphone. "Friends! Here me now! The disappearance of our daughter, Jenna, is not an isolated occurrence. This event is but one of several tragedies that has befallen this community of late. Satan has arrived in Seven Hills! 'Then it goes and takes along seven other spirits more evil than itself, and they go in and live there; and the last state of that man becomes worse than the first.' The spiritual doors of this community have been left unsecure by the open worship of the occult. Because of this, evil has been allowed to creep in and has found a happy home among the Pagan rituals and false idols. Jesus has been forgotten.

Now is the time to stand up to Satan and to tell him that evil has no place in Seven Hills! Now is the time to tear down the false idols of Pagan worship and renew our faith in our Lord and Savior, Jesus Christ! Now is the time to not only be prayerful but militant in bringing others in the community to Jesus! Now is the time we must fall to our knees and ask the Lord for forgiveness, to bring our Jenna home and to save the rest of our children from Satan's clutches! Now, my friends, is the time! Will you join me in praying for Seven Hills?!"

"Let us pray," David added.

Paster Thomas returned to his place in front of the microphone, looking a bit shell-shocked. "Let's bow our heads…" he began, and I stopped listening, realizing my heart was thumping in my chest.

"Now might be a good time to leave," Tara reasoned, motioning to the parking lot. We nodded and quietly slipped from the crowd, candles still in hand, as Paster Thomas delivered a solemn prayer into the microphone. We could hear his echoing voice even after we closed the doors to Theo's station wagon.

Once we escaped the maze that was the overcrowded parking lot, Tara's voice broke the silence. "What the fuck was that?"

"Nothing good," Theo responded. A line in her jaw ticked, and I wondered if she was clenching her teeth. "At least not for us."

I turned and looked out of the window into the darkness, at the trees as they flew by, wishing to be a bird that could simply fly away.

Chapter 3

I woke up at 6 am still exhausted. I had tossed and turned all night, thinking of the events of yesterday: the search, the confrontation with Cliff and his very public accusation, the strange end to Jenna's candlelight vigil. According to Cliff, we, the Culpepper sisters, had something to do with Jenna's disappearance. We snatched her from her car and, potentially, locked her in Culpepper Manor. Who knows what ungodly things we did to the poor girl from there. I knew in common lore, witches ate the young, and used them to gain longevity and power. A young girl, possibly stranded, close to our property would have given us the perfect opportunity to strike.

Throughout the night, watching the minutes tick by as I laid in bed, I thought of all the things I should have said. The accusations I should have hurled back. I should have discussed Cliff's money laundering, his shady dealings, revealed to all he was involved with VanHoy and Mills. But, instead, I froze in the moment, only asking—a plea—that my sisters and I be allowed to stay. To help. The thought of this exchange infuriated me. Burned me until I sweat through my pajamas and onto my sheets.

Memories of the vigil also replayed in my mind. Jenna's mother's outburst. The desperation in her voice as she described Satan's influence in Seven Hills. The growing anti-Pagan sentiments in town frightened me, even if my rational brain knew there was likely only a small minority of people that agree with her harsh words.

But, as Ronnie pointed out at Seven Sweets, tragedy could be a recipe for spiritual manipulation. I thought of the accused witches of long ago—women who thought, perhaps, their own town, their own people, would not turn on them until it was too late. I thought of the allegory of the frog sitting in the pot, as the cook slowly turned up the heat, realizing too late that he was, in fact, boiling.

And lastly, I thought of Jenna, just 16, practically a baby out there, alone, missing—and who knows what else now. Almost 72 hours gone. I had watched enough *CSI* and *Criminal Minds* to know that the first 48 hours in a missing person's case were crucial, and we were past that now. From the search, we knew that she likely did not walk or run into the woods, leaving only one possibility: she was taken.

Still lying in bed, I took what I intended to be a cleansing breath, but all I felt was unease. Dread. I wanted nothing more than to take a mallet to my head, as characters did in the old *Looney Tunes* cartoons, and knock myself out clean. I desperately needed a break from thinking, and being knocked out cold seemed to be the only way I could accomplish that.

Despite my fatigue, I got out of bed. I wondered if it was some sort of trauma response that, when my world is in chaos, I feel the most motivated. In times of stillness and calm, I can barely move. Stillness and calm make me nervous; the day feels too vast and too much can happen. In times of chaos, the bad thing has already happened. Missing girl. Check. Town suspicion directly pointed towards us. Check. Public confrontation in which accusations are made. Check. Check. I grabbed my phone. A text from Ronnie read, "I hope you're okay." I turned my phone over without replying. *Already ignoring his texts*, I thought, guiltily. *You're doing it again.*

I decided on a warm, fleece hoodie, and a pair of black yoga pants as my uniform for the day. Then, I sloppily tied my dark hair into a bun. I had made a silent and secret pact to myself that I wanted to keep. I was to become The Magician—someway, somehow. And part of becoming The Magician was confronting the truth about my family, the truth that was *apparently* hidden in the house.

I did want to know, once and for all, as Tara had expressed, what happened. If for nothing else, for my own peace of mind. I could not allow outside noise like Cliff Bishop, Brent Silverton, Donna Dickson, anonymous commenters, or anyone else in this town to derail me. One thousand accusations could be hurled at me and my sisters, and I would stand tall, as my mother instructed me to do. I walked over to Tara's bedroom quarters, flipped on the light in her sitting room, and opened her bedroom door without knocking. As I pushed the door open, the light showed into her room and into her blue eyes.

"Seriously?" she mumbled before rolling over. "What apparition is in your room now?"

"Shut up," I clapped back, sitting on her bed. "I was thinking... maybe we should search the grounds?"

"For Jenna?" Tara asked groggily.

"No," I growled, annoyed. *We would absolutely know if Jenna was on the grounds.* "For stuff..." I made my voice bolder, "For mysteries of the Culpepper women. Aunt Elaina said everything we need is right here in the house. Theo is probably already at The Alchemist. I want to do an unsanctioned search."

Tara laughed and sat up slightly, propping some pillows behind her. I could see she was wearing one of her favorite night shirts. An oversized t-shirt with the phrase, "DON'T YOU WISH YOUR GIRLFRIEND WAS HOT LIKE ME" emblazoned in all capital letters across it. Tara was always just so... Tara, even when sleeping.

"What are we searching for? Information or dead bodies?" she asked, following a long yawn.

"Answers," I replied, and then shuddered. All we needed was to come across Jasper's remains today. I pushed the thought from my mind. Of course he wasn't here. He couldn't be.

Tara sighed. "Yea, okay. I guess. I am tired though. Was up sexting all night with some guy from a dating app."

"Ew," I cried, disgusted. I grabbed a stuffed animal at the end of her bed, a pastel pink hippo, and hit her with it. "No need to share that. Alright, come on. Let's go."

I left the room to let Tara get dressed and walked downstairs to the utility closet. I grabbed a couple of flashlights, testing each one to ensure it worked. Luckily, I found two flashlights that worked, although one of the bulbs was quite dim. I was searching in vain for extra batteries when Tara arrived downstairs a few minutes later.

"Alright, let's do this!" she exclaimed. "But why the flashlights? Can't we *just* turn on the lights or are we trying to get the full experience?"

I ignored her questions. "I was thinking we could start with the root cellar?" I posed, tentatively.

"You are dead wrong if you think I'm going down into the root cellar," Tara declared dramatically. She made a motion like she was going to turn around and abandon the mission.

"Fine. I'll do it," I mumbled, and she turned back around. I wondered what the point of a little sister was, if you couldn't force her to do your bidding. I, unfortunately, had never been able to force Tara to do anything, let alone my bidding.

Tara and I moved in silence as we exited the front of Culpepper Manor, the wind howling as we closed the door. I looked up, taking it all in as we walked. The house looked ancient in the still darkened morning, haunted, full of secrets. No wonder people thought we could—or might—hide bodies, dead or alive, here. I shook my head to remove the thought. I wondered what we would find in the root cellar. It was an original fixture of the house, once used to store food and wine. These days, we rarely entered it. I do not know the last time one of us crawled down there. The root cellar seemed to be the perfect place to hide, and possibly, find things. What kind of "things," remained to be seen.

"So why do you think Mom and Aunt Elaina hid all of this shit?" Tara asked, cupping her hands around the flashlight and breathing into them.

"I don't know. Maybe they thought, after Jasper went missing, the police would search our home? Maybe they didn't want family secrets just lying around? Maybe they were worried their stuff would be taken by the police and never returned?" I posed the questions in rapid succession.

"But what information do you think they were hiding? What couldn't the police see?"

I turned to look at her, our breaths visible and suspended in the air. "I really don't know."

"Do you think Theo knows more than she is letting on?"

I thought about that for a moment. "Possibly," I answered honestly.

There was a strong possibility that Theo was trying to protect us—or maybe even protect herself—from the truth. I knew it would do a number on Theo's psyche to find that Mom and Aunt Elaina, were, in fact, murderers. Again, I pushed the thought from my head, trying to focus on the task in front of me. *Keep your head where your feet are*, I said internally, a phrase I learned from a YouTube video on how to stop catastrophizing. I spent an entire January several years back, binging pop psychology videos in the hopes of bettering myself. At least one "trick" stuck—sort of.

In the early morning, it still felt like winter outside, and I felt regretful for not wearing more layers. By the time we reached the side of Culpepper Manor, less than one minute later, the bottoms of my yoga pants were soaked. *I should've put on boots too*, I thought to myself, annoyed at my own stupidity.

While it was still frigid feeling, the temperatures had warmed over the last couple of days, melting the snow on the ground and in the trees. There were a couple of patches of snow still standing, and most of the ground was wet and muddy. I could feel my tennis shoes slightly sinking into the ground with each step. I looked around, taking stock of my surroundings. Branches and other debris littered the property. This in-between stage was the least flattering: the snow was gone, but it was not yet green.

"It's too cold!" Tara complained, pushing her sleeves up over her hands and regripping the flashlight. We paused for a moment, both looking at the large, wooden double doors leaning against the root cellar.

"Well, open it," Tara demanded, crossing her arms. The light of the flashlight flicked across the yard, fading before it reached the woods.

"Help me," I urged, grabbing one of the thick wooden doors and pulling as hard as I could. The wood was cold, wet, and slimy. I should have worn gardening gloves. This was probably why it was better to do a sanctioned search involving Theo: She would have planned ahead; probably would have prepared muffins in celebration of the search. Or, would she have shot us down, encouraged us not to look, protecting herself just as much as us from the truth about our family.

Tara did not move to help with either door, but we both used our flashlights to peer down into the root cellar after I had pried them open. We could not see the entire space, but we could see enough to reassure me that there were likely no wild animals living below. At least not wild animals of the larger variety.

"Do you think that ladder is even still stable?" Tara questioned, as we flicked the flashlights into each corner of the root cellar.

"I guess there is only one way to find out," I responded. I handed her my flashlight and turned around. I leaned close to the ground, and tentatively lowered one foot onto the ladder. There were only about six steps, and I comforted myself with the knowledge that I would likely not fall far if the ladder should break. One foot on the first step. Then two. Then, I tested out the second rung. Slowly, testing each rung along the way, I made my way to the muddy dirt floor.

"Throw me a flashlight," I ordered. "The better one."

Tara threw the flashlight down, not a far feat, as I lifted my hands in the air. The root cellar smelled like a fresh grave: earthy, muddy, and slightly woody. Each side of the cellar was outlined with old wooden shelves. I scanned each shelf quickly with the flashlight, but paused when I heard a faint scratching sound.

"I think there is a mouse down here!" I exclaimed, now searching the ground below me with the flashlight.

"It would be more shocking if there wasn't," Tara retorted, her outline only visible in the light of the flashlight. "I don't know why this couldn't wait until the sun came up. Don't get bitten by anything weird. I am not in the mood to take you to the hospital."

I rolled my eyes and began my task, taking my time. There wasn't much on the first set of shelves directly across from the ladder. A hammer, and a corroded spool of twine decaying into the wood, a large jug full of a dark substance. Probably wine. I hoped, and then shuddered for the second time today. It reminded me of blood, a sight I hate. There is just something so grotesque to seeing something that should remain inside on the outside. I reassured myself that, of course, witches didn't drain their victims of blood. That was vampires. Witches and vampires. Maybe I wasn't just tired and anxious; maybe I was on the verge of hysteria.

When I felt satisfied there was nothing of note on the shelves directly in front of me, I turned my attention to the shelves to the left, pushing cobwebs out of the way with my flashlight. A bucket stood below the shelves, empty, except for a thin layer of grime covering the bottom. On the bottom shelf there were some gardening tools, antique looking and rusted, next to them a decomposing umbrella—or was it a towel? Then, a set of relatively new looking keys. I aimed my flashlight at the keys. Their lack of shine indicated they had been down here for a while, although probably not as long as many of the other items.

"I found a set of keys," I called to Tara. "I am going to throw them up. So watch out."

I grabbed the keys tentatively, holding the cleanest part of one of the keys between two fingers and launched them up onto the grass above the root cellar.

Tara walked away from the root cellar, probably looking to inspect the keys with her flashlight. She returned to the top of the root cellar.

"I don't know. It looks like someone just hid spare keys to the house and whatever else down there."

"Well, I want to check them out. Put them in your pocket while I inspect the rest of the shelves."

"Ew, no. You," Tara, instructed, shining her flashlight in my eyes. "Haha," she spoke rather than laughed.

"Mature," I muttered and turned to continue my examination of the shelves. Other than a few odds and ends, nothing seemed to be of particular interest. I slowly climbed the stairs and lifted myself out of the root cellar. This time, Tara helped me lift the doors back into place. I grabbed the keys from their place on the ground, holding them outstretched like they were contaminated.

"I don't think the keys are really anything," Tara announced again, as we rounded the house.

"Probably not," I agreed. "But we have the rest of the property and the house to search. Are you going to help me?" I asked.

"Depends on the mood I'm in," she responded, and I believed there was never a truer statement spoken.

The Magician

The Alchemist was eerily quiet when Tara and I arrived around 9 am. I guess, after the events of yesterday—the confrontation, the hushed voices, the whispers—we were reentering into a phase in which we were very, very familiar: social pariahs.

"Has anyone been in?" I asked Theo, after hanging my coat on a hook behind the register.

"No," Theo responded, "Not even Deidra." Theo looked worried.

"Well, it's still early," I offered. "Listen, don't worry so much about it. It is what it is."

"We had a note on our front door," Theo divulged, grimly.

"So?" I asked, "What did it say." I knew before I even asked the question that it was going to be bad. "Fuck," I muttered under my breath.

Theo went behind the counter and opened the register. She handed me the note. Scrawled in spiking lettering, the note read:

> Die Satan's whores.
> I know you had the girl.
> Drank her blood.
> You are filth and God will punish you.

I looked at Theo, horrified. "Are you fucking kidding me?" I asked, aghast, my hand involuntarily moving to cover my mouth.

Tara came up behind me and read the note over my shoulder.

"Sometimes I feel like these idiots could really do better," she muttered.

"Did you contact the police?" I asked Theo.

"Should I? I mean, really, should I?" I thought about all the events of last year. At times, it felt like all the police did was make matters worse. I absolutely did not want to get caught up in this investigation.

"I don't know," I looked at Tara over my shoulder. "What do you think?"

"I say fuck all of them." Theo and I looked at each other, ignoring Tara's input, searching each other's face for how to proceed.

"Maybe, I should call Ronnie?" I offered.

"Treasure, seriously, what the hell is Ronnie going to do?" Tara implored, angrily.

"I really don't know," I stated, bewildered. "Just help, I guess."

"So, what, you guys can go all Scooby Doo again and almost get your ass killed?"

"Tara STOP!" Theo yelled.

Just then, we heard the sleigh bells, and all three of us whipped around to face the door. A customer, an older woman dressed in sensible slacks and a purple winter jacket, stood in the doorway looking at us, startled. She looked at each one of us for a long moment before walking right back out of the door without ever turning around.

"Not on the floor!" Theo exclaimed, throwing her hands up. "We can't afford to lose any business right now."

"Theo, for the love of all things, stop catastrophizing!" Tara exclaimed. "This is all probably not as big of a deal as we're making it!"

"Okay, okay," I said, trying to calm everyone down. "Let's think about this rationally. We received a threatening letter. Why don't we just let Chief Dodd know?"

"You're right," Theo replied, looking visibly calmer. She took another deep breath in. "That's a good idea. He'll know what to do, and he always seems to have our best interest at heart."

"Treasure, take it to the station," Tara ordered.

"Are you kidding me?" I gaped at her. "I can't go in there. I am already basically dodging their calls."

"Nobody cares about that anymore," Tara stated, rolling her eyes.

I rolled mine right back. Tara was so obtuse at times. Of course, people still cared about the biggest murder case in, perhaps, Seven Hills' modern history. And unfortunately, due to my untimely entrance into Mrs. VanHoy's home, I was now a part of that case and its lore. Not to mention, I was already a part of Jasper Alden's case and its lore. I did not want to become a part of the Jenna Bishop case. I wanted to avoid everything about it.

"I'll take it," Theo offered, annoyed. "Honestly, you are both insufferable at times."

Theo took the letter to the station and didn't return to The Alchemist for the rest of the day. She texted us that we were to finish out the day and close the shop. She was going to get McDonalds, and then take the rest of the day off.

"Didn't even offer to get us anything," Tara stated, after reading the text from our group chat aloud, annoyed.

The Magician

Tara and I worked for a couple of hours in silence, only speaking to greet and check out customers. At around four o'clock, I offered to let her leave so she could go get her own McDonald's. It turns out, it was just that sort of day.

"I'm going to text you if things get crazy here," I warned, as she gathered her things.

"Knock yourself out," she responded, which was not quite an agreement.

I took a deep breath when she left, grateful to be alone. Taking advantage of the slow day, I busied myself with dusting shelves, cleaning windows, and disinfecting surfaces. I even carved out twenty minutes to clean the computer we kept at the register, meticulously cleaning the keyboard with a Q-tip. Despite Theo's wishes, maybe I would close and lock up early tonight, get my own comfort food, and turn in: curl up with a good book and completely zone out.

At around 5 o'clock, the bells on the door clanged, and I looked up from the register counter to see—Detective Harrison. I stood there looking at him, stunned for a second. He was dressed in a crisp white button-down shirt, a suit jacket, and perfectly tailored black pants. I felt entranced, unable to move or speak. He cracked a smile. A smile I had nearly forgotten about in the almost half a year since I had last seen him. I suddenly realized I was staring and tried to snap myself out of it.

"I hope you have a warrant," I called to him, working to keep a smile off my face, looking down, making a concerted effort to remain neutral in face and body.

"Naw, I'm here on a personal call," he mocked, a bright smile on his face. He walked towards me keeping eye contact, until he reached the register counter. He relaxed his body, leaning forward, close to me, resting his elbow on the counter. The smell of mahogany flooded my nostrils. I had almost forgotten that smell.

"I see. What can I do for you then, Detective?"

I immediately regretted the words as they left my mouth. There was no real way to say "what can I do for you then, Detective" without sounding sexual. I might as well have offered to give him a blow job. Heat spread through my body until it reached my face.

He smiled again. A broad, wicked smile. "I wanted to look around. See what's for sale."

"See what's for sale," I repeated, skeptically, nodding slightly, making a faux "thinking" face.

"Yes, you see, I love to shop. Where are the rest of the Culpepper women?" He grinned broadly, smoothing his hand down his expensive-looking shirt.

"They left," I stated, matter-of-factly, and then sort of regretted it. I remember when Theo, Tara, and I were younger, our mom and Aunt Elaina would caution us to never answer the door when we were home alone. We could answer the phone but must never reveal that we were by ourselves. "Say we are on the grounds or otherwise cannot come to the phone. Never ever say you are home alone," my mother cautioned. I wondered if I should have told Harrison that Theo or Tara were on the grounds or even in the shower. I smiled to myself.

"So, I have you alone?" Harrison teased.

I nodded. "Kristy Pickles would be scandalized."

Harrison threw his head back and laughed. "There is a woman I hadn't thought about in a while."

Seemingly, Kristy Pickles' full time job was carrying information from person to person all over town. I tried to rack my brain for her actual job and came up with nothing. Maybe gossiping truly was her full-time job. She brought me a fair amount of information about Harrison last year, mainly his womanizing. I wondered what information she brought to him about me. I knew that, whatever it was, it was likely not good.

"Don't think about her—and don't say her name, especially into the mirror," I warned.

He chuckled again. "So, how are you doing?" he asked, almost without mockery.

"Off the record?" I teased back.

"I've yet to Mirandize you."

"Something to look forward to," I stated, and I could be mistaken but it looked like the detective may have been a little flustered. He opened his mouth to reply and then closed it again. "What are you looking for, Detective Harrison? Don't tell me you came all the way over to 'Satan's Den' to inquire about my well-being."

"Well, I did," he said, crossing his hand over his heart, pretending to look hurt. "I heard there was a little bit of upset at the search."

I nodded, trying not to wince.

"What aren't you telling me?"

"You think you can read me so well after only a handful of encounters?" I questioned, jested, really.

I didn't want to talk or think about the search, especially after having a couple hours of break from over-analyzing the situation. I wanted to keep things light. Normal. And this was what Harrison and I, apparently, did: spoke in riddles and mocking tones.

He paused and removed his jacket, and I watched as he began to roll up his shirt sleeves. I tried to look away, as it was virtually pornographic to look at his tanned, muscular forearms. I felt heat spreading through my body again, remembering my drunken antics at The Witches Brew last year.

"You're loitering," I deadpanned, wondering if he somehow knew exactly what he was doing with the forearm peep show.

"You're right," he responded, standing up straighter, a grin on his face. "I better get what I came for."

Harrison slowly went through our inventory and picked out a couple items. I studied him from the register while he examined each item, maddingly gorgeous even in profile. He, indeed, looked as if he knew exactly what he came in for.

I slowly scanned each item. A satchel filled with herbs for protection, a crystal for healing, and incense used to cleanse a space.

"Interesting items, Detective. What aren't *you* telling *me*?"

He looked me in the eyes and smiled broadly. "Until next time, Treasure."

Harrison exited the store, bells clanging in his wake.

Chapter 4

A storm was coming. Clouds knitted overhead as I drove the winding road out of town and back to Culpepper Manor, just beating the rain as I pulled into our long driveway next to Theo's old Chevy Caprice. I had decided to close The Alchemist up early, but I had failed to procure any greasy fast food for myself. *I'll just raid the fridge when I get home,* I had decided as the trees along the highway whipped past me. I had been speeding, windows down, feeling the cool air whip through my hair. I felt truly energized for the first time in days, maybe even months.

After I killed the ignition, I sat in the car for a few minutes when it began raining, hard. I sat mesmerized for a while, watching the rain slip down the windshield. *What a day. Detective Harrison back in Seven Hills.* I pulled my jacket around my body tightly, bracing to exit the car and enter the rain that now poured freely from the sky. Fat droplets fell on me, soaking my hair, my coat, my purse, as I ran to the front door. I opened the heavy door and practically ran into Theo and Tara.

"Treasure!" Theo exclaimed, looking awestruck. "We heard your car door."

"What?!" I bleated, a sense of alarm filling my body. Something was off. *What could it be now?*

"Holy shit, Treasure. You will not believe what we found in the attic! Tara exclaimed, staring at me, shaking her head.

"What?" I inquired, my heart quickening.

"We found it all! What Aunt Elaina told Theo about!" Tara exclaimed, grabbing my arm and pulling me.

"What? Where?" I demanded.

Theo seemed to regain her composure. "The keys you and Tara found in the root cellar. One of the keys unlocks a filing cabinet in the attic."

"Okay?" I asked, confused.

"You just have to come up and see," Tara hinted, excitedly.

The three of us made our way through the house and then up the narrow stairs and into the attic, a floor we seldom set foot on. I could feel Theo and Tara's excitement, so palpable, the air had become electric, buzzing. My whole body was practically humming as we entered the poorly insulated and seldom-touched space, my wet jacket and clothes clinging to me.

The hairs on the back of my neck stood on end and goose pimples spread down my arms and legs. I remembered why we rarely went up there. It was creepy. And cluttered. And dusty. On each side of the floor, sheets covered old furniture and boxes coated with a generous layer of dust. Twice, I felt as if I had walked through a spiderweb, as we bobbed and weaved through the storage.

Finally, as if we had reached the gold at the end of the rainbow, we came to a relatively new-looking filing cabinet. The keys were positioned in the lock. Tara and I stepped away from the cabinet as Theo opened a deep drawer, showing folders labeled "tax returns."

"Okay?" I asked again, not fully understanding this reveal. "Is there something in the tax returns?" I could already feel the dust coating my nose and mouth. I sneezed into the wet elbow of my jacket.

"They're not tax returns," Theo began to explain. "Well, the first couple of documents are. I saw the keys you both found on the counter in the kitchen. One of the keys looked like it might belong to this filing cabinet. I only recalled the cabinet because I remembered Mom and Aunt Elaina taking boxes and boxes of things up to the attic not long after Jasper…" she cleared her throat, "went missing… I also thought it was strange there were tax returns in here. We keep all of the tax records at The Alchemist. Of course, I thought there was a possibility they were duplicates, but when I started pulling the documents out, we found…"

"Okay, so what is it?" I cut Theo off, my heart pounding now. Now was not the time to be long-winded.

Theo slowly pulled out the tax folders and laid them on the ground. It was clear that Theo and Tara must have wiped off a spot when they were up here before I came home. There was a circle-shaped clearing of the dust on the floor. On top of the folders, Theo began laying out what appeared to be notebooks and journals.

"What is all of that?" I questioned, incredulous.

"It looks to be grimoires, books of shadows, other odds and ends," Theo answered, as she continued to reach into the drawer. "We started going through some things but wanted to wait for you to be with us to fully look through everything. Some of the writings were obviously done by Mom and Aunt Elaina," Theo added, "I recognize their handwritings. But, some… are… clearly… from other people."

"What other people?" I questioned.

"Our ancestors? Perhaps, members of a coven that they belonged to?" Theo theorized, wiping her hands on the apron she was wearing. Why was Theo constantly in aprons? I thought she took the rest of the day off.

"Were Mom and Aunt Elaina in a coven?" I queried.

"I'm not sure," Theo admitted. "But I think there is a good possibility they were."

A memory, once again, returned to me. My mother and Aunt Elaina chanting, as I peered through a crack in a door:

> *Grant my wish*
> *Grant my desire*
> *I shall achieve all I aspire*
> *I already have what I require*

I had so many questions about this memory. Where were Mom and Aunt Elaina? How did I get there? Was I spying alone or was Theo, and maybe even Tara—although she likely would have been quite little—there as well? Were Mom and Aunt Elaina chanting alone or could they possibly have been with others—a coven?

"I have a memory. One of Mom and Aunt Elaina chanting," I explained, relaying the chant. "Do you guys remember it? The chant? Or them chanting?"

Tara shook her head, looking a little sad, a rare emotion for her. "I don't remember."

A knife-like pain twisted in my stomach, remembering just how young Tara was when all of this started happening with Jasper. She was probably too little to really remember *before* Jasper disappeared, before our lives were turned upside down.

I kneeled and picked up an old blue leather book Theo had placed on one of the tax-return folders. It was quite small, almost the size of my hand. A brown leather strap was wrapped around a button on the front. I slowly unwound the strap, as gently as I could, fearing the cover and button might detach from the papers inside. As I opened the book, just as I feared, the papers began to slide from the spine. Adjusting to sitting cross-legged on the floor, I looked through some of the pages, careful not to touch anything with my wet clothes. At a glance, each page seemed to be covered in cursive writing. I tried to make out a couple of sentences.

The gate is locked. But the gate is imaginary.

I read the words aloud, looking over at Theo and Tara, who were also rifling through notebooks.

"What the hell does that mean?" I implored.

"No idea," Theo responded. "The gate is locked but the gate is imaginary?"

"Weird," Tara remarked. "I wonder how long it would take us to go through all of this stuff. There is more in the other drawers as well. Let's take all of this downstairs to the kitchen table," she suggested. "I can't breathe up here."

As if on cue, my mind flashed, as it seemed to do frequently now, to the time I couldn't breathe—Hansen's large, red hands around my neck. I could barely remember Hansen's face on *that day*, but what I did recall vividly was his sunburned arms, peeling so badly he looked like he was molting. The smell of alcohol on his breath. I shivered again, feeling weighed down by my still-damp clothes, and tried desperately to push the memory from my mind. I suddenly felt trapped in the small area. I stood up quickly, startling Theo and Tara.

"You alright, Treasure?" Theo asked, peering at me, concern etched on her face.

I nodded. "Yeah, I just want to go downstairs."

As Theo and Tara made their way to the kitchen, items from the filing cabinet in hand, I made my way to my room for a scalding hot shower and to hang up my wet clothes. I was still buzzing. Journals, grimoires, books of shadows. We had stumbled upon what was probably our birthright, our heritage, what might be our legacy.

But who to leave it all to? We were the last of the Culpepper women. Last of the Culpeppers. Possibly the last of the witches in this area, if you could even call us that. We were now just novelty-store owners, a part of the cog of the tourist wheel, and nothing more, capitalizing on Witchcraft without actually practicing it in a meaningful way. My sisters and I probably, when it came to the craft, did not do much more than the casual new-age influencer: journaling and dabbling in tarot and crystals.

By the time I rejoined Theo and Tara at the kitchen table, warm pajamas on and my hair in a topknot, the contents of the file drawers were laid out neatly on the table. There were so many books, papers, and strange objects that almost all of the large cherrywood kitchen table was covered with the contents. I scanned all the items. Many of the notebooks were newer looking, but others looked as though they might fall apart if touched. I spotted the blue journal I had flipped through in the attic, sitting on the far corner of the table.

The objects Theo and Tara retrieved from the filing cabinet were equally as awesome as the dozens of handwritten books. A corn husk doll, a gold chain holding a pentagram, a fancy altar knife with a jeweled handle, a bottle of what appeared to be sea salt, an aged deck of tarot cards, a homemade tarot deck that was faded and handwritten on paper, some dice, and a few rocks and crystals.

A black velvet purse. I stared, remembering the story. Our ancestor, Sarah Culpepper, if the stories were to be believed, beat a Witchcraft charge by casting a spell that involved putting a cow's tongue, tucked away in a black velvet bag, beneath a judge's chair. I picked up the purse and began feeling around for any lumps, when satisfied, I opened it to reveal it was empty.

"I already checked!" Tara exclaimed, laughing merrily. "The first thing I did."

"Whoa," was all I could manage to say as I put the purse down and made a couple more laps around the table, examining all the items. There was so much: it was overwhelming.

"We made a few trips to the attic, and we didn't even grab it all," Theo announced, her eyes moving up and down the table.

"Did you see the jar, Treasure?" Tara asked, pointing to Theo.

Theo stood up from where she was seated and held up a jar in her hand, near the antique light fixture that hung over the table.

"What the hell is this?" she implored to no one in particular and squinted.

Tara and I both stared at the object. The Mason jar was full of reddish liquid and something else—something I couldn't quite make out. She passed the item to me. I also held up the jar to the light. It was filled with water. In the water sat what appeared to be a piece of paper. At the bottom of the jar lay what looked to be a red ribbon, disintegrating.

"Paper and ribbon?" I hypothesized aloud, watching some of the bits bobbing and floating in the jar. It was like a homemade, discolored, snow globe.

"Paper would have completely dissolved," Tara stated, as I handed the jar to her. She was right. There is no way paper would have lasted… who knows how many years. "But what the hell is it?" She wondered aloud. Theo took the jar from Tara's hand, examining it from the bottom where the ribbon sat.

"Should we open it?" Tara asked.

"I'm almost afraid to open it," I uttered. "What if it like… unleashes… something?"

"Like what?" Tara asked.

"I don't know. But already… it's been… strange… I don't know… lately."

"You know," Theo started, "I've been in the root cellar. Last year, at some point. I forget what I was even looking for, but I never saw those keys. I mean… I can't be sure, but I think I would have remembered if they had been there."

"But how did they get there?" Tara asked. "A ghost?"

I could physically feel the blood draining from my face. Something had been in my room, sitting in my chair, disturbing my sleep, leaking on my floor.

"Could we ask Ronnie? You know... about the jar?" Theo suggested. "He is educated on... this sort of thing."

"We could bring him the jar and see if he would look at it? Suggest what it might be?" I posed. "We might have to open it though."

Tara physically bristled, "How do we know we can really trust Ronnie? I don't think we should let him in on all of this. He writes books, publishes articles. This is *our* family, *our* life. We don't need more attention..." her voice trailed off. "Especially right now, you know with Jenna going missing and the whole 'Satan's whores' thing."

The photo of Jenna Bishop's smiling face flashed in my mind. The young girl was just gone, seemingly into thin air, not unlike Jasper, our father. *Was there some sort of Bermuda Triangle right here in Seven Hills?* I closed my eyes and envisioned people walking through the town square and then just disappearing, never to be seen again. I shook my head.

"I don't think Ronnie's into the whole 'Satan's whore thing,'" Theo countered.

Tara smirked, "He would be if Treasure was into role-play."

"Oh my God, Tara!" I shrieked, as she laughed.

Ever the adult, Theo redirected the conversation. "What if we just ask him about the jar? We don't have to tell him about anything else. At least not yet, and not unless we want to."

"I can say I found the jar in the house, and that is all," I added.

"Fine," Tara agreed, rolling her eyes up to the ceiling.

"What's your issue with Ronnie?" I asked, feeling slightly annoyed. Tara seemed to pick and choose who she liked and did not like at random. When she decided she did not like you, nothing you ever did was right.

Tara shrugged. "He's just so boring."

"He's not," I corrected, and then I guiltily remembered Ronnie's text, checking on me this morning. My promise when we painted the hare and egg was not to be a stranger. Already, I was failing him. It's just that so much happened today. I then blurted, "Detective Harrison is back."

Tara looked annoyed. "For what?"

Theo looked up from the notepad she was flipping through. "How do you know?"

"He was at The Alchemist," I admitted.

"For what?" Tara asked again, this time looking angry.

"I don't know. Shopping. It was odd. He bought a protection spell satchel, selenite, and palo santo."

"Really?" Theo questioned. "That's so bizarre."

"Could it have to do with Jenna's disappearance or the note we got?" Tara questioned.

I shrugged, "I really have no clue."

"I don't know, guys. But I do know we have a lot of work to do tomorrow for Ostara, and it's getting late," Theo said, tiredly.

"Is Ostara... still... a go?" I questioned, wondering if the community would still celebrate with a young girl missing and a broken mother declaring that our Pagan traditions opened the door for Satan's influence.

"I really don't know." Theo wiped her hands on her apron and then smoothed back her dark hair. "But we should be prepared regardless."

"You're right," I said, standing from my own chair. "It's getting late. Why don't we all go to bed and talk about this in the morning."

Tara grabbed two of the books, "I'm taking these to my room. I'm going to start going through them."

Theo nodded. "Fine. Just don't lose anything."

"I want to too," I stated, grabbing the small blue journal and another newer-looking black journal. The journal had a shiny, black, plasticky cover with two gold prongs; holding it shut was a tiny gold lock, the key wedged inside. It looked like a child's diary, something you might buy a 10-year-old to stuff in their Christmas stocking. Who wrote their deepest darkest secrets, assuming that is what the contents were, in a child's diary you could likely purchase at a Value Mart? I guess this was modern day Witchcraft.

"Well, let's keep the jar down here." Theo said, holding up the object and examining it again. "Treasure, ask if Ronnie would like to meet tomorrow to look it over. Let's see if we can figure out what it is."

When I was downstairs, I had been exhausted, but now, I laid in bed, wired, unable to sleep. For the third time in the last hour, I checked my phone: 11:30 pm. I rolled onto my side and turned on the lamp. It was official; I was giving up on sleep. I sat up and grabbed my phone, still plugged in, cradled it in my lap and texted Ronnie. I thought about texting him *"You up?"* the classic booty-call question, smiled to myself, and then thought better of it.

Ronnie and I, while we had been around each other with a fair amount of frequency, at least last year, had never crossed the line into flirtation, although we did share one lingering hug around Halloween. Sometimes, as Tara had indicated downstairs, I felt as if he might want more. But I never felt like I had more to give. I imagined Ronnie, the studious, semi-famous scholar, falling in love with me. *Me.* The woman who could barely get out of bed, often for weeks-long stretches. I vacillated, but ultimately decided to text him:

Me: We are doing okay. How are you?

I waited for a few moments to see if an ellipsis would appear and nothing. Ronnie was probably one of those that powered down his phone before he went to sleep and slept soundly—the sound sleep of the "untraumatized."

I knew of Ronnie's parents, his mom. She had always seemed nice, normal. She probably never chanted with her sister under the cover of night, and she most certainly didn't murder Ronnie's father.

Ronnie's father was still alive, still living with his wife. He probably went to work, went home, and then retired to the easy chair, paper in hand, asking his wife what was for dinner. Or maybe this was my sitcom understanding of what a father was, what a father did. Despite Ronnie's and my friendship, I knew very little about his family life. His life. I had never been to his place. I had never asked, never even imagined where he lived, what he did when he wasn't with me. I was a selfish friend, naval-gazing at my own trauma.

I got out of bed and crossed the room to the open French doors. I scanned my sitting room, and when I was confident nobody and nothing was there, I entered. I sat on the chair, the same chair where an apparition had sat only nights ago, and I picked up the blue journal. Opening it carefully, I looked at the first page. The name "Edith Daisy" was scrolled on the blank page. I scanned my brain for the name. *Edith Daisy. Edith Daisy. Was Edith Daisy a Culpepper or was she a friend—possibly a member of a coven long ago?*

I wondered if Ronnie, in his work on the occult, might know who Edith Daisy was. I began flipping through the pages. Crooked, cursive handwriting covered each page. Quickly, I realized this was a spell book. There was a spell for rain. A spell for love. A locator spell. Even a spell for indigestion that involved eating ginger. *Well, that's just cheating*, I thought and smiled to myself. I tried to read the words for each spell as I came upon them, but much of the writing was faded or illegible. I imagined Edith

Daisy, hurriedly scratching these words as she went about her day.

I closed the book and picked up the plasticky black diary. I turned the lock in the key, flipped it open, and, sure enough, scrolled on the first page was a name: Diana Isla Culpepper.

> *Bless this book*
> *And all inside*
> *From all enemies shall it hide*
> *So mote it be*

A tingle of energy ran down my spine. My mother. I turned the page.

> *Elaina is angry with me. She can't believe I've kept this secret from her. But I have my secrets, as she does. This is one of my worst qualities: secret keeping. My mother used to call me "the squirrel", hiding little secrets, like nuts, away for later. Everything between Jasper and me is so intense.*

I gaped at Jasper's name. My father. And continued reading.

> *I know Elaina won't understand and doesn't want to understand. She hates him. And I, I am obsessed with him. Body and soul. The first time I met him, I knew I was a goner. I am a goner now.*

Again, I gaped. So, my mother *did* love my father, and she didn't just love him: She was obsessed. I scanned my brain for any memory of them together. Nothing. I kept reading.

> *I promised Elaina I wouldn't see him anymore, especially now. But, I can't stop.*

I flipped through the pages, pausing on a passage.

> *He bruised my wrist. I couldn't let Elaina see, so I wore long sleeves for a week. I suspect she knows but says nothing.*

What the hell? Who bruised my mother's wrist? I flipped through to read the entire passage. Jasper. He had grabbed my mother's wrist during an argument, bruising her. I closed the book for a moment. Now, I see why Mom and Aunt Elaina decided to hide all of this from us and, perhaps more importantly, the police. This would certainly not look good. The word "*motive*" flashed in my mind.

I flipped through a couple more pages. More passages about Mom and Jasper's fucked-up relationship. Is this why she kept him away from us? Was she protecting us? But, why would she keep seeing this guy, and not just seeing him: reproducing with him? I never thought of my mother as anything but a solid person. I had so many memories of her spending time with us, reading to us, teaching us, encouraging us. She was the mom of all moms. Truly.

The woman in these passages seemed so unlike my mother. Spellbound and love crazed. No mention of Theo, Tara, and me in these passages. Only Aunt Elaina. *Were we born yet or was she so caught up in this relationship that she failed to mention us at all?* Of course, I had only skimmed some of the pages. The entire journal was filled. Maybe we were in there somewhere. I felt disturbed, queasy. I was not sure I wanted to know this information.

I stood up and walked out on my balcony, overlooking the woods. The cold air blasted through the door as I opened it, shocking my system and cooling what was rapidly turning into a throbbing headache. I had forgotten to eat in the midst of all the excitement. In my hand, I still held the tiny, gold key to the journal. I thumbed the hardware over and over again, when a thought occurred to me. I stood on my tiptoes and chucked the key as hard as I could into the woods, not bothering to look to see where it may have landed.

I said aloud, "If I am meant to know, may the key come back to me."

I promptly went back into my room and locked the journal. I was freezing now, my feet feeling like two blocks of ice.

Suddenly, a sharp chirp interrupted the silence, and I gasped. I giggled nervously when I realized it was my phone. I had a text.

Ronnie: I am glad. I'm doing okay.

I suddenly felt sharply and acutely lonely. I thought about texting Ronnie, asking him to come over. Would he? I wanted arms around me, someone to spoon me, coddle me, baby me. Someone to distract me from what I had just learned.

Me: Can we meet up tomorrow? Maybe for breakfast? I want to pick your brain about something.

Ronnie: Yes, of course. Seven Sweets?

Me: What time?

Ronnie: 7 am? You're the one that's wide awake. It's almost 2 am.

Me: That works. Couldn't sleep. Why are you awake?

Ronnie: I fell asleep at 9 pm. I just woke up and saw your text.

My thumbs thrummed over the alphabet on my phone. I debated what to say next.

Me: And you decided to text me back right away? Flirty.

Ronnie: I always text you back right away.

Flirty back. I paused and debated again.

Me: I'll see you at 7.

Ronnie: See you then.

I turned my phone over, before I texted anything stupid. I switched off my bedside lamp, and I was plunged back into darkness. And like a moth to a flame, my mind drifted to Detective Harrison, dressed in that crisp white shirt, leaning on my counter, face close to mine. *Obsessed*, the word my mother had used. They say curses are generational.

I closed my eyes and dreamed. In my dream, Jenna is lured into the woods by a shiny, black, plasticky apple. She takes a bite of the apple and falls to the forest floor. Long green fingers grab her. Drag her. Take her further into the woods. She disappears.

Chapter 5

The alarm on my phone chirped, indicating it was 6:00 am. I sent a text to Theo and Tara, letting them know I would be at Seven Sweets with Ronnie. I went to my bathroom and splashed water on my face, examining my tired eyes, and decided to add some foundation to my face and a little mascara. Lipstick seemed too much for 6 am. I changed from my pajamas into a suitable outfit: black leggings and a red, comfy, oversized, turtleneck sweater. I gave my hair a quick brush and threw it back up into a topknot. I took another look in the mirror. I still looked tired, but I looked significantly better. On autopilot, I walked down to the kitchen, to the table, and grabbed the Mason jar. I took another look at its floating contents before putting it in a tote emblazoned with "The Alchemist" logo. I walked out the front door.

For the first time this year, it smelled vaguely like spring. I took a deep breath. The air smelled like rain, grass, dirt, and a slight crispness I couldn't quite identify or describe. Droplets of rain were still clinging to the newly revealed grass and pine needles, making everything appear greener, more vibrant. The wet woods sparkled in the moonlight, looking like a gleaming sapphire jewel. Green from one angle and brown from another. Soon, spring would be in full force, making the woods lush and inviting. I thought of the tiny gold key, out there somewhere, and wondered if I should look for it before I left. Obviously, I could not have thrown the lightweight object very far. But I didn't know if I wanted to find the key, wanted to know more about my parents' tumultuous relationship. In the end, I decided to just get in my car.

The morning was so incredibly still and tranquil that I almost regretted disturbing the peace when I turned the key in my ignition. As I reached the end of our driveway, I noticed a car had pulled off the highway and was parked on the edge of our property about a half of a mile down the road. I swallowed. The car was parked about where Jenna's vehicle was found. My heart rate picked up a bit. *Who would park there? Are they a part of the camp that suspects we might be involved in her disappearance? A part of the camp that believes we are Satan's whores, women who confer with the Devil and grab young girls from cars?* Tara was right: These idiots really could do better.

I made a snap decision to turn right, towards the car, instead of left, into town. Apparently, I was ready to confront the car's owner with nothing on my person but a small handbag and a Mason-jar-filled tote. I imagined myself swinging the tote bag with the Mason jar over my head like a weapon and laughed out loud. Perhaps, the driver will assume I am crazy and leave the premises. As I neared the parked car, I noticed it was a basic late-model government sedan. Detective Harrison. It must be. I killed my headlights as I pulled up behind his car, putting my own car in park. As I opened my door and exited, I noticed him at the edge of the woods, flashlight in hand. He was not in his usual attire, but instead was wearing dark blue jeans and a navy hoodie.

"Detective Harrison?" I called, almost questioned, walking closer to him.

He looked spooked, whipping around and shining his flashlight in my eyes. I held up my hand to shield my face.

"Detective Harrison. It's Treasure."

He put the flashlight down and hustled towards me with long, almost elegant, strides.

"Treasure, what are you doing here?" he asked, looking genuinely perplexed, examining me from head to toe.

"I live here. You're veering very close to being on my property." I pointed in the direction of Culpepper Manor.

I regarded him. He looked tired, like he hadn't slept all night. Even in the moonlight, I could see he had little wrinkles at the edges of his eyes. I imagined it might be difficult to sleep when you are a detective and a young girl is missing.

"I saw your house. I'm quite impressed," he responded, again, genuinely. What happened to all the mockery? The jeering? The sarcasm? Was it too cold and too early for such exchanges?

"Why are you here?" I inquired, but I already knew. He must be getting a feel for the landscape, the traffic, where one might go if trying to run.

"I'm working," he stated, matter-of-factly. "Trying to figure something out... for myself."

"What are you trying to figure out?"

He smiled slyly, revealing two rows of perfect, white, square teeth. The Harrison I knew starting to shine through. "Treasure, if you try to get involved with this case, I might have to kill you myself."

I laughed. "I'm not involved in this case. I'm staying as far away as possible. Trust me. Especially after the search and what I witnessed at the vigil. I don't even want to be a concerned citizen anymore."

He chuckled, sighed, shoved his hands in his hoodie pocket, looked at me pointedly, and smiled that toothy smile again. *Damn. Did he always look this good so early in the morning?* His smile faded and he looked deep in thought for a couple of seconds, the silence stretching between us. We were both breathing heavily, little puffs of air visible in the cold, morning air.

"I wonder if you can help me though, with a few things."

"If you think I'm setting foot in the police station..." I began.

"No, I mean like answer a few questions for me, if you have the answers. Nothing formal. Just a few things about this area, the items in your shop, the community, that kind of thing."

I studied him. "For what?"

He shrugged, casually. Almost too casually. Practiced. Was this some sort of police trickery?

Were we suspects in this case as well? Would he trick me into implicating myself—my whole family? People were falsely accused and convicted of crimes all the time. This was practically the origin story of Seven Hills.

"For my own information. I'm interested in learning about Seven Hills, and it might help me with everything that is going on. I assume you might be the right person to ask, considering you and your sisters have lived here your entire lives."

"Actually, maybe ask Ronnie Jackman. He's a historian; might be better." Then I added, "He's a doctor."

"I'm not asking him, I'm asking you."

A tingle shot from the back of my neck down to the base of my spine.

"Fine, when and where?" I tried to seem nonplussed. I could also be a practiced casual.

"Is there a bar around here... other than the Witches Brew?" he implored, chortling a bit.

"Depends on how far out of town you want to go," I responded.

"Truthfully, I want to get as far out of town as possible. But I'd settle for the nearest establishment that sells drinks and maybe some mozzarella sticks."

I laughed, "Harrison, I'm shocked. I pegged you for a 'protein only' type of guy."

"Stop," he smiled, and I thought, again, he looked cute. In the early morning. Dressed like this. He still looked tired but seemed younger than usual. Lighter. I imagined this was sort of what he might have looked like as a boy: handsome, playful, comfy, free of worry.

"There's a bar if you follow this road straight." I pointed in the opposite direction of downtown. "Sort of a trucker-type place."

"I've seen that place."

"Yea, but I doubt they have mozzarella sticks; although I do hear they still allow you to smoke inside, despite the laws."

He snorted. "Sounds like quite the place."

"Well, I'm definitely not going into the Witches Brew. The owner of that fine establishment tried to kill me, remember?"

"Yes, but based on his performance at the station, I would say he is much more afraid of you than you are of him," he rubbed the slight dark stubble on his face and then smiled widely, a wicked smile, never breaking eye contact.

"He's full of shit," I stated flatly.

"Name the place, Treasure." A soft command.

I considered this. *Could we go into Seven Sweets? Maybe the new restaurant in town, Boil and Broom?* I thought about Deidra seeing us, my sisters potentially seeing us, and I didn't like that idea. I didn't like the idea of others in town seeing us either. And the thought of Kristy Pickles seeing us—well, that thought made me feel sick.

"Why can't we just go to your place?" I blurted, before I fully realized what was coming out of my mouth.

He looked mockingly scandalized. "Treasure," He slapped his hand over his heart, "What will the neighbors think?"

"Well, listen, I can't go with you to a public place, and you can't come here," I said, motioning towards

Culpepper Manor. "Because my sisters hate you. We can't go to Seven Sweets for the same reason, plus Deidra. That basically leaves the dive bar up the highway or the McDonalds' drive thru, so what do you think?"

"All those people really hate me?" he asked, looking good-humored, but slightly incredulous.

Who could hate the sexy detective?

I cocked my head, gave him an annoyed look, but then couldn't help but smile.

"And what do *you* think about me?" he inquired, teasingly, emphasizing the word *you*, making it sensual.

Heat traveled to my face, and I took a deep breath, blowing it out in one fast "whoosh."

"Do you want my help or not?" I checked the phone in my hand, 6:30 am now. "Because I have a place I need to be."

"Avoiding the question, I see," he mocked. "You can come to my place. But I will warn you it's not much of a place. I don't even feel at home there. Do you want me to pick you up? Say about 7ish?"

"No, I'll drive, but I need your address." He gave me an address for an apartment in town and his phone number.

"Let me know if you chicken out," he teased.

I rolled my eyes. "You seriously have problems."

And just like that, I had my very own secret to squirrel away.

Ronnie was already sitting at a table with Deidra when I walked into Seven Sweets.

"Good morning!" I cheered happily.

Deidra smiled, "Well good morning! You're in a good mood for being up so early."

"Yea," I uttered, suddenly feeling a little self-conscious, and sat down. Seven Sweets smelled so incredible: like chocolate, cake batter, spice, and coffee all at the same time. "So how are you?"

Ronnie already had a cup of coffee in a bright, teal mug sitting in front of him. I watched the steam rise, as Deidra filled us in on the goings-on of Seven Sweets. It was doing incredibly well. Her business picked up after the events of last year, when more looky-loos started showing up, and it had remained steady ever since. She explained that she was even considering expanding.

"That's incredible," I exclaimed. "Think of how far you have come since you started!"

She did a little mock squeal. "Ah, I know! I'm just excited. So, fill me in on what this meeting is about."

"Okay," I started, extracting The Alchemist tote bag from my side. "My sisters and I found something strange last night."

I placed the tote bag on the table and pulled out the Mason jar, placing it in the middle. Both Deidra and Ronnie's eyes narrowed, examining the object.

"Can I touch it?" Ronnie queried.

"Of course," I responded, pushing it closer to him with my fingertips.

"Where'd you find it?" Deidra asked, looking a bit awe-struck.

"It's creepy, right? In the house, in the attic more specifically," I answered. Then I asked Ronnie, "Any clue as to what it might be?"

"I don't know," he muttered, seemingly mostly to himself. "Can I open it?"

"It's funny you ask that," I commented, trying to sound light. "Theo, Tara, and I were debating that last night, considering whether we should open it. We were wondering if it would like... I don't know... unleash something."

Deidra looked slightly alarmed. "Like what?"

"I don't know," I admitted. "Maybe I've watched too many Ouija-board horror movies or something." I guiltily realized that I hadn't yet told Deidra about the apparition in my room. I needed to catch her up on that, on everything we found in the attic, what I read in the journal, and maybe even Harrison. Maybe.

"We could never sleep after watching those!" Deidra exclaimed with a chuckle and then stood. "I have to get back to work. I'll let you two talk. Do you need anything before I go?"

"Maybe a banana nut muffin? And a cup of coffee, of course. The dark roast," I ordered, always feeling slightly odd asking her to wait on me.

"Of course. Ronnie, anything else?"

"You know what? I'll have a banana nut muffin too."

"Coming right up!" she announced, turning on her heels. She seemed brighter today. Happy. Maybe my good mood was contagious. I watched her as she hustled to the back to retrieve our food and coffee. Meanwhile, Ronnie continued to study the jar.

"Is this the only thing you found?" he asked, pausing his examination to make eye contact with me.

I paused for a moment, remembering my conversation with Theo and Tara. "Yes. That's it. Up in the attic."

"Hmmm. I think I have an idea of what it might be. Do you have time to head to my office with me?"

Just then Deidra returned with our muffins and my coffee.

"I hate to do this," I said apologetically to Deidra. "But could we possibly get everything to go?"

Ronnie and I arrived at Seven Hills Town Hall mere minutes later, in our respective vehicles, both of our coffees in to-go cups and muffins in hand. Last year, I discovered Ronnie had an office in the town hall, when waiting to talk to VanHoy's secretary about the mayor's whereabouts. Now together, we were coming to his office with a new mystery to solve: *What is in the bizarre Mason jar?*

Ronnie's office was as neat and tidy as I remembered it. He took a seat behind his desk, and I plopped into one of the uncomfortable office chairs in front of it. He was studying the jar again.

"I'm thinking we should really take this to the lab at the University. Really take a look."

I grimaced. "I'm sorry, but I'd rather we didn't. You know this being my family's and all... I was really just wondering if you could give me some ideas... you know... off the record."

He looked uncomfortable for a second. Maybe he was considering what this object might truly mean, how it might relate to the "goings on" with my family, if you will.

He simply replied, "Of course."

From a filing cabinet, Ronnie pulled out a large plastic mat. The sort of mat you might put under a kitchen sink if a leak sprung. He removed a large paper calendar, a pencil box, and a shiny, metal apple from his desk, before setting the mat down on top of the surface.

"Moment of truth," he teased, setting the jar on the mat. When he unscrewed the jar's lid, it let out a slight "pop" from the built-up pressure. Using a pair of unusually long tweezers, which he also must have retrieved from the filing cabinet, he carefully pulled out the piece of paper floating in the middle of the jar and placed it on the plastic mat. Then, also with the tweezers, he fished out the mostly disintegrated red ribbon.

"You know what? I do think I know what this is!" he exclaimed, sitting back in his chair, looking excited.

I literally moved to the edge of my seat.

"What?!"

"I think it's a banishing spell."

"Why? What makes you think that?" I inquired, feeling a bit defensive. The feeling seemed to come out of nowhere with no prompt. Maybe I didn't want to think my mother and aunt would do such spells? I didn't have time to overly analyze my emotions before Ronnie continued.

"Well, I remember reading about banishing spells some time ago, while doing some research on modern Witchcraft. This is sort of a modern-day binding, where you take a Polaroid of the person you want to bind, literally bind them up with string, usually with some fun chants, put them in a jar, fill the jar with water, and pop them in the freezer. Voila! Your enemies are on ice and can no longer do you harm. But this was in the attic, right? Not the freezer?"

I nodded. But it really didn't matter. The object could have been removed from the freezer, may have *needed* to be removed from the freezer. How would it look if the police searched our home and a sworn enemy's photo sat in our freezer, bound by string?

"You think your family had an enemy, enemies?" Ronnie asked, seemingly without thinking.

Then, we made eye contact, my heart constricting. My voice sounded weak, barely audible, barely mine, as I responded, "Yes, I believe they did."

And the town believed they did too. Jasper Alden. Our father.

I hope I didn't seem insane in Ronnie's office, I thought, as I splashed water on my face in the bathroom of town hall. For a moment in Ronnie's office, I could feel a panic attack coming on, crashing over me like a wave. Things were starting to add up, take shape, an awful inhuman gray shape, causing me to look at my mother and Aunt Elaina in new ways.

Every trace of Witchcraft was hidden in our home. Throughout our entire childhood, we were raised in the tradition. It was essentially the center of our everyday life. Then, I realized suddenly, when Jasper disappeared, it was hardly ever brought up again. An unfinished sentence. Almost like we were never *truly* practicing at all. My mother and Aunt Elaina had motive to kill Jasper. He harmed my mother, at least once that I knew, left bruises on her wrists, and according to my mother's own writings, my Aunt Elaina openly hated him and likely knew that he left bruises on my mother's delicate, pale, wrists. Now, we find a relic, a physical sign, that efforts were made to protect us all from someone. And not just someone—an enemy.

Of course, that enemy could be Jasper or could be anyone, I rationalized. *Did they have a lot of enemies in this town or was Jasper the only one?* Of course, this could be a good thing too. We were taught to work with energy, work with nature. Perhaps, Mom and Aunt Elaina felt like they couldn't act, and spell work was their only recourse. Their *only* course of action. This would mean that nothing was physically done, and all was left to energy and fate.

Under the harsh lighting, I stared at myself in the mirror for what felt like a long time. I had promised myself that whatever the answer was, I would face it. I attempted to clean myself up by wiping my eyes and the rest of my face with a scratchy, brown paper towel from the paper-towel dispenser. My mascara was now smudged underneath my eyes, making me look deranged, feral.

I took a deep breath, and I indulged in a new thought. What if Mom and Aunt Elaina had murdered Jasper? Did it really need to change how I felt about them—how I still feel? Of course, it did, right? Good, decent people would care. Denounce their relatives. But others in town didn't denounce their relatives. I thought of Cliff Bishop, Jimmy Dickson, and even Hansen Mills. Of course, however, money laundering, police cover-up, and even choking a young woman were not as bad as murder, right?

I physically forced myself to leave the bathroom. I found Ronnie back in his office, looking concerned.

"You alright?" he implored. "Don't take this the wrong way, but you look a bit ill."

"I'm fine," I mustered and gave a small smile. "Thanks so much for your help."

"You know, banishing or binding spells are really common. So many people do them, even for something as innocuous as, my students would say, bad vibes."

I laughed a little, feeling a bit better.

"I have a student who tells me she does them all the time! Even if she passes someone in the grocery store who seems a little off."

"Wow, where does she keep her pizza rolls?"

Ronnie snickered and then his face dropped a bit. He looked at me square in the eye. "Treasure, I have something to tell you." He looked like he was about to rip off a Band-Aid. "My mom has been talking to me about the goings-on of some people over at

Trinity Church. She tells me that there is a faction of people that are getting a bit extreme over there... I guess."

"Okay." I shifted uncomfortably in my chair. "What do you mean by extreme?"

"Just like the anti-witch sort of rhetoric. She feels, headed by Donna Dickson and Cliff Bishop's mother, Valerie, there is some sort of mission to get rid of our celebration of witches and 'Pagan-esque' themes in town. And of course, Kristen Bishop, Jenna's mother, seemed to echo a lot of those views at the vigil."

"But do we really celebrate witches or Witchcraft?" I challenged, with a bitter laugh. "Sure, we do fun, sort of corny, names to honor our history and there is All Hallows' Eve—but we all know those women weren't witches. They weren't stealing the manhood from men in town. They were women trying to live their lives, maybe living off the beaten path a bit for the time, but they were harmless. What wasn't harmless was all the hysteria that left five innocent women dead."

"I totally agree," he acknowledged. "I just think, especially given Jenna's disappearance, this is really bad news. My understanding is they are whipping up some members of the congregation into a frenzy. They are having meetings at the church about protesting the Ostara celebration and even some businesses in town."

"What businesses?" I demanded, already knowing the answer.

"Essentially all businesses with names 'glorifying the occult.' But, yes, of course, The Alchemist as well. I hate to say this, but The Alchemist is basically public enemy number one. I thought you should know."

I sighed and sat back in my chair. When I didn't respond, Ronnie continued, "I guess Donna and Valerie have formed a friendship and are now front and center in the drama surrounding our 'Pagan history.' They are constantly going on about how the Devil has corrupted our town and our values. Basically, Valerie and Donna are using our town's 'association' with the occult to excuse their sons' misdeeds. Cliff and Jimmy did nothing wrong, but people—the whole town along with the Devil—are trying to bring them down sort of thing. And, of course, with Jenna's disappearance…"

Ronnie's voice trailed off, but I could 'get the drift.' Without Ronnie having to say it, I knew when he said, "the whole town along with the Devil," he really meant me and my family. I wondered if Donna Dickson, Valerie Bishop, or even Kristen Bishop, in the midst of everything her family was going through, put the note about Satan's whores on our door. Or maybe all three of them did it together? Girls' night on the town.

"We got a note," I explained, relaying the contents of the note to Ronnie.

Ronnie looked devastated. "I am so sorry, Treasure."

"I'm starting to think maybe I should leave Seven Hills, maybe even leave the country. I have roots in England and Ireland. Maybe I could start over somewhere over there, buy a small cottage, open a little shop. I don't know."

I thought of Aunt Elaina out there somewhere. Wandering. Or maybe not wandering. Maybe living in a little cottage with her own little shop, a little "The Alchemist" pop-up, if you will. Nothing but her plants and the odd customer to keep her company. The thought sounded wonderful at the moment.

"You can't leave," Ronnie said shyly, almost verging on sheepishly. "Seven Hills would be so boring without you."

To my surprise, The Alchemist was busy when I arrived around 9:30 am. When Theo saw me walking through the door, she looked relieved.

"Can you please restock the shelves?" she practically begged, while walking to the register to check out customers.

I busied myself restocking, organizing the back, and even mixing up more cleaning products from our all-natural, homegrown ingredients, when I got time to breathe. The Alchemist was so fragrant now, several people walked in just to inquire about what we were working on. This gave us a needed sales boost, as most walked away with our homemade products.

We were both happy to see Tara walk through the door at around 1:00 pm, although she did not look nearly as happy to see us. "Have either of you checked the news?" Tara held her phone up to indicate she had read the news on her phone.

"No, it's actually been a great morning here," Theo told Tara, looking relieved. The Alchemist was less busy now. There seemed to be a lunchtime lull. Perhaps, people were taking a break from shopping to eat some lunch or skipping lunch to head over to Seven Sweets to pick up a midday lemon buttercream cupcake with lemon zest sprinkled on top. My stomach growled, and I thought of the uneaten banana nut muffin in the back of The Alchemist. The muffin that traveled from Seven Sweets to town hall to here: largely untouched. I could hardly believe it was only lunchtime. So much had happened today, that it felt like multiple days packed into one.

"More information has been released about the Jenna Bishop case," she explained, her voice low as to not disturb the lone customer still perusing the shelves.

"Did they find her?" I asked, hopefully.

Tara shook her head. "No. Not that I know of as of right now. But I read an article that suggested she must have been taken near where her car was left. I guess a couple stopped, an older man and woman, when they saw the car, talked to her, and offered to help. Even called the police. They left, and by the time the police got there, she had disappeared. Poof." Tara threw her hands up in the air as if she was performing a magic trick.

"So, there was only like a 10-minute window in which she disappeared? It never takes the police long to get anywhere here. Did the article offer if she seemed inebriated or otherwise altered?" Theo inquired.

"According to the article, the couple said she seemed normal. They felt comfortable enough leaving her there, knowing the police were on their way," Tara disclosed.

"That is so weird. So, either she completely left and wandered somewhere far enough away that people could not find her, or someone grabbed her in that short amount of time?"

Tara nodded. "It's creepy."

Theo added, "Even creepier that it was so close to the house, while we were sleeping."

"If she had gone kicking and screaming, do you think we would have heard her?" I questioned, really considering this. Culpepper Manor was enormous and almost surrounded by woods. Would it be possible to hear Jenna's cries in the night if she had made them? Or would the woods absorb all the sounds, all the energy, taking it in like one living, breathing, entity.

"I really don't know," Theo responded finally, and Tara shrugged in a sort of agreement.

We paused our conversation to check out the last customer. After the bells clanged, I took a deep breath. I needed to fill them in on everything—well, almost everything. I started with Ronnie's assessment of the Mason jar, which I had reassembled before packing it back up and leaving for The Alchemist. Neither Theo nor Tara seemed that shocked or that alarmed.

"What if they put Jasper on ice?" I asked, still in a hushed voice, although The Alchemist was now empty.

"So what if they did?" Tara answered, unbothered. "Maybe he deserved it. It still doesn't mean anything."

"Well, I have something else to tell you both. I read parts of one of Mom's journals or book of shadows. I'm not quite sure what it was. According to her own writings, she was obsessed with Jasper. And well... he hurt her... at least once. He grabbed her wrist and bruised her. She also wrote that Aunt Elaina hated him, probably knew that Jasper had harmed her or at least suspected it. I was so distraught I threw the damn key to the journal out of the window."

Both Theo and Tara looked at me awestruck.

"Why did you throw the key?" Tara demanded.

"I didn't want it anymore. I didn't know if I wanted to know about them... all the details about them. It sort of felt wrong to read? I don't know."

"So, you just chucked the key out of the window?! What about if we want to read it?" Tara yelled.

I rolled my eyes. "Tara, it's a journal you can get at a Value Mart. I'm pretty sure, if we really want, we can bust the lock or cut it off. No problem." I paused, collecting myself and lowering my voice. "I don't know. I just wanted a sign, I guess. Maybe a sign from Mom. That it is time for us to know this information."

Theo was silent. Too silent.

"Theo?" I questioned, looking at her.

And that's when we heard it. Chanting. But not the chanting from our childhood. Not melodic voices in unison, using sound to create energy. Chanting, like sing-song chanting, attention-seeking chanting.

Like a school of fish, we all moved from where we stood to the front window of The Alchemist to see a group of about 10 people, mostly women, walking down the street. They held a blue banner that read "Repent Sinners: Save our town!"

Some business owners had exited their shops. I spotted Paul Richards, the owner of The Craft, a small craft store across the street, standing with his son, Pauly, watching the spectacle. A woman from the group paused when she saw him and handed him a flyer.

"Should we go out there?" Tara queried.

Theo shook her head. "No, absolutely not. Hopefully, they'll do their little demonstration and leave."

"What are they chanting?" I implored, signaling for my sisters to lower their voices.

I strained to hear, pointing my ear towards the window, but was still unable to make out the words. I turned my head to see Paul, leaving his son and jogging over to our store.

The bells clanged as he walked in.

"I couldn't help but notice you all huddled in the window," he chuckled, moving to stand at the counter by the register. "I've been hearing things here and there, but it turns out they are getting crazier over at Trinity Church... shame too. It is such a beautiful place, has always been lovely every time I've attended. I don't think it's really the church itself. Pastor Thomas is great. I doubt he would agree with or condone this little demonstration."

I nodded. "I just spoke to Ronnie Jackman today. His mother regularly attends, and she said the same thing."

"What does the flyer say?" Tara asked, moving to the counter to peer at the piece of paper. She picked it up and began reading: "'We have indulged in Witchcraft long enough in this town! We must repent or risk losing it all! Resist sin and save our town!'" She paused, looking at all of us. "There are some Bible verses at the bottom too. 'Don't turn to psychics or mediums to get help. That will make you unclean. I am the LORD your God.' Leviticus 19:31. There are a couple more scriptures on here as well."

We all looked at each other, awestruck, and a little embarrassed. The whole display was a bit cringeworthy. Did they really think celebrating the town's history was, in itself, Witchcraft? Couldn't they see that history was, at least to some extent, repeating itself right here in Seven Hills? Once again, some in town were choosing to go after beliefs that differed from their own. And as we all should have known by now; this could have dire consequences. I thought of the five women hanged, thought of my ancestors, my mother, Aunt Elaina, the note. Us. I thought of last year. People assumed we had murdered VanHoy because, what, we were different? This was getting a bit out of control.

Paul laughed again, "Must be why so many in the church are trying to get these people removed? People come in complaining all the time. 'The church never used to be like this.' From what I hear, most of the congregation are not happy with this rhetoric or the proposed protests. It sounds, and frankly looks like, just a small few are supporting this 'cause,' if you can call it that. I just hope it doesn't run that church into the ground."

I nodded, comforted to know that most did not believe in the message displayed in town here today.

"What were they chanting?" Theo asked, moving closer to where Tara was holding the flyer.

"Something about 'Cast a Spell' and 'Go to Hell,'" Paul shook his head as he relayed their rallying cry. He laughed merrily again. "It's just so incredibly ridiculous. Everyone knows Witchcraft isn't real."

Chapter 6

Thankfully, the rest of the day was uneventful, and The Alchemist stayed busy. Perhaps, the situation was not as dire as we originally thought. Maybe we just had a couple of slow days, and we were not social pariahs after all. Harrison sent me just one text throughout the course of the day, reading "8 pm?" I told my sisters I was going to Deidra's. I wasn't sure why I needed to lie—or more accurately, wanted to lie. It seemed too complicated to explain why I wanted to see him, and I didn't even quite understand it myself. Or, at least, I did not want to admit why I wanted to see him, not even to myself.

The evening was unusually dark when I left The Alchemist: A starless sky, making it seem later than it was in actuality. It took me less than 5 minutes to drive to and to find Harrison's apartment complex. It was a small complex with just a few buildings, past Seven Sweets in the opposite direction of Culpepper Manor. I had briefly considered going home after leaving The Alchemist. Showering. Changing. Gussying up, and then doubling back. But it seemed ridiculous to come all showered and fresh faced when he essentially just wanted to ask me a few questions about the town and The Alchemist. It seemed embarrassing. I couldn't have him notice this and mock me for it all night. The time I came over all dressed up so he could ask me what sage was. I'm not sure I could live down the mortification.

After locating his exact building on the lot, I entered, looking for his apartment number down a long hallway that smelled vaguely like cat and a synthetic 'fresh linen' scented plug-in. I found unit 6B and knocked on the door. He answered looking tired, casual, and slightly tussled. His hair looked a little wet, like he had showered not long ago. He smelled amazing—like mahogany, and I wanted to shove my nose in his neck and breathe it in. Like in the early morning, he was dressed in a pair of dark jeans and hoodie, this time a light blue one. The color brought out his eyes.

"Treasure!" he exclaimed in a fake cheerful manner, while holding the door to his unit open to let me in. "So nice of you to drop by." He smiled broadly, ushering me in with his hands. I took a few steps inside.

His apartment looked almost shockingly bare. There was a brown leather couch, and a TV hung on the wall. No TV stand underneath. One lone cord cascaded down into an outlet below. I also realized there was no coffee table, no end tables, nor any other furniture. No art on the walls. No blankets. No throw pillows. Past the living room, there was a small kitchen, visible from the little countertop that separated the two spaces. Most people would probably put some bar stools there, but no such stools lived there now. There was no dining area, no dining room table, no chairs.

"You live here?" I asked, looking at him, smiling, looking for him to confirm. "It looks like a person with no fingerprints lives here."

He guffawed at that, pinching the bridge of his nose with his thumb and pointer finger, his signature sign of frustration. I was annoying him already. "What? You don't like it?" He nudged my arm playfully with the back of his hand.

"Give me a tour," I demanded, mostly so I could memorize the contents for later. His place, the sights, the smells, would give me something to think about when lying in bed.

"Well, we're already in the living room," he gestured to the sofa and TV. "Follow me to the kitchen."

He led me the few steps into the small kitchen. A yellow and green sponge sat on the metal sink, and there was a small round bottle of hand soap, lemon scented, and nothing else on his counter. Nothing else in the space. Not even a hand towel hung from the oven door. The counters and all the appliances appeared to be immaculately clean. There was no evidence that anyone had so much as prepared one piece of toast here.

I nodded at him and uttered a "nice."

He grinned broadly. "Bedroom!"

I followed him as he led me into the only bedroom. There was one dresser and a neatly made bed, topped with a navy-blue comforter. A single nightstand held a lamp and his expensive looking wallet that I remembered from last year, when he drove me to McDonalds to grab a cup of coffee and accuse me of writing a fake article about VanHoy. I smiled to myself.

"Gorgeous," I commented, looking over at him. "I love what you've done with the place."

He laughed, "I don't really live here. I'm more squatting here."

"Where do you really live?" I asked and followed him from the bedroom back into the living room area.

"Another pretty bare apartment in Boston. But it is a step up from here."

"I always pictured you living in a high-rise surrounded by granite and stainless-steel appliances," I admitted. "With maybe a hot blonde on your couch, ready to do your bidding every night."

He chuckled so merrily it made me smile. "You couldn't be more wrong. Although, I like the part about the hot blonde. *That* sounds *really nice*. Especially the whole 'doing my bidding' part." He raised his eyebrows at the 'doing my bidding part.'

"You're sick," I responded, but also grinned.

"You brought it up!" he protested, and then leaned in close to whisper in my ear, "Although I like the part about *you* imagining *me* more."

My whole body went slack at that, his breath tickling my ear. I felt deliciously languid. Relaxed. Like I downed a whole bottle of wine prior to my arrival.

"So, what questions do you have?" I blurted, feeling suddenly hot.

"Always business," he mocked. "Come sit down." He gestured towards the leather sofa.

He perched on one side and I on the other.

"You need some blankets and throw pillows," I teased. "Make it feel more 'lived in.' We have hundreds at Culpepper Manor."

"Culpepper Manor? Your house has a name?"

"Doesn't yours?" I mocked.

"I guess... 6B?" he responded, and I laughed.

"Bring me some," he urged then, his blue eyes fixed on me. "Blankets and pillows."

We lingered in silence for a few moments, intentionally not looking at one another.

"I feel weird," I admitted, smiling at him. And I did, but a good kind of weird. Excited.

"Me too," he agreed, and he slid his hand across the smooth leather material towards mine and touched my fingernails with the pads of his fingers. His touch felt surreal, electric. Goosebumps covered my limbs and my stomach squeezed. I felt like I should pull away. Resist in some way. This was, most likely, an incredibly bad idea. But I didn't pull away. I just continued to look at him. He gripped my hand then, tugging a bit, pulling me towards him.

And then his lips were on mine, soft. Harrison was kissing me so crushingly soft and slow that I felt like I couldn't breathe. My hands moved to find purchase. They landed on his biceps and then on his large shoulders. And then I was straddling him, kissing him so hard I worried for a moment I might suffocate him. His hands were on my hips around his lap, and then under my sweater on my bare waist. I was shamelessly grinding against him, searching for friction. We stayed like that for minutes, hours—maybe even days, kissing, kissing, kissing, until, finally, he lifted me up and carried me into his bedroom.

I moved my face from where it was shoved into a pillow to turn and look at Harrison. We were both naked, under the covers, and his large hand was playing with my hair that was now a knotted mess down my back, having escaped from my bun sometime during the last hour.

He grinned when I looked at him and continued his petting, pulling the strands slightly, making my scalp tingle, and causing goosebumps to spread down my arms and legs.

"What were you doing out by the woods by Culpepper Manor this morning?" I asked, although, of course, I had already asked, and I already knew. I felt desperate to fill the quiet, suddenly feeling nervous, vulnerable in my bare state.

I immediately regretted the question because he stopped playing with my hair, stopped touching me, and propped himself up on his elbow, looking at me. He looked so unbelievably sexy, like a model in a cologne ad, that my breath hitched for a second.

"I wanted to get a feel for the area. How busy it is. What's around there. In your experience is there a lot of traffic on that road? Do you hear a lot of street noise from your home?"

"It's never really that busy," I responded, considering this. "Truly. At any time of the day. Theo, Tara, and I talked about the night Jenna disappeared. We were wondering if we would potentially hear someone 'kicking and screaming,' so to speak, if there was a fight between her and an attacker. But we all weren't sure. We know we didn't hear anything that night, but it's hard to know if we would have. The woods out there just sort of absorb everything."

"It's kind of creepy out there," he admitted, smiling lazily.

"It looked like I startled you this morning."

"Yea," he paused. He seemed to consider his next words, and then said, "You know... I kept thinking I heard things in the woods... I know this sounds insane... but I thought I could hear... I don't know... chanting."

The hairs stood up on the back of my neck.

"What kind of chanting?" I exhaled out, breathlessly.

"I don't know. It was the strangest thing. Sort of hard to describe. At first, I thought I could hear people... sort of like... murmuring faintly." He rubbed his jaw with his free hand. "But then it sounded like there was a rhythm to it. I know this sounds strange. But that's why you saw me on the edge of the woods. I was trying to listen. I don't know. Maybe it was just so quiet out there I was hearing things." He paused again, considering his words. "I feel like strange things happen when I'm here. We aren't that far from Boston, but it almost feels like another world altogether."

"Yes," was all I could think to say. "That is creepy."

"So, tell me about your store, The Alchemist." Rapid change in subject.

"Well, it's been in my family forever. We just sort of sell fun things to help people get into the 'Seven Hills spirit,' if you will." I made my voice sound light. This was the very vanilla version of what The Alchemist is to me and my family, who my family is and has been in this town. I just couldn't imagine telling Harrison the infamous Sarah Culpepper cow tongue story, and I especially could not imagine telling him in the *nude*.

"And what would you say the 'Seven Hills spirit' is?" he jeered.

I laughed and rolled on to my back, pulling the comforter up and beneath my chin. "You know, kitschy, witchy, cozy, that type of thing. I mean even *you* are getting into the spirit. Have you used anything you bought?"

"Okay, hold on," he said, reaching over me, moving over me, and past me, to the nightstand by the bed. He opened the top drawer and grabbed a few items in one hand. He kissed my lips and then my neck on his way back to his side of the bed we were currently sharing. "What do these things mean?"

He spread the items from The Alchemist across his pillow. I saw the familiar protection spell satchel, the selenite, and the palo santo. I sat up slightly, pulling the comforter up with me, looking down on him and the pillow.

"Well, a protection spell is exactly what it sounds like. Selenite is used for so many things, or more accurately, can help draw certain energies into your life. It will help you attract peace, mental clarity, healing, all of that. Palo santo is used for smudging..."

"Smudging?" Harrison fixed his gaze up at me. "What the hell is smudging?"

I laughed, "Like cleansing. You use it to go through your space and remove all the bad energies... or even old energies... sort of like 'break it up.' Why did you pick these items out?"

I could see him thinking. "I was curious... and maybe I wanted an excuse to go in there."

My stomach flipped.

"Alright!" he announced, suddenly jumping up and out of bed. I watched him, completely naked, looking like a work of art, covered in muscle and scars. Seeing his scars made me wonder about the botched raid Harrison had been part of as a detective in Boston that almost got him killed. At the time, Harrison had a partner, Detective Joel Miller, who, unbeknownst to Harrison, had been in cahoots with some of the local drug dealers that they had been investigating. During the raid, Detective Miller had shot Detective Harrison in his side, narrowly missing his heart.

Thankfully, Harrison had been able to flee to the basement and escape through a window before Miller and others could reach him. Detective Miller shot himself in his own home before he could be arrested. I had never asked Detective Harrison about this incident; I only knew about it because of a random Google search I had conducted after we first met. Still, I wondered what he would say about it and if I even had the right to ask.

I studied his body as I watched him tug open a dresser drawer and pull out a pair of basketball shorts. If he was self-conscious about his scars, it was undetectable. He slid the shorts on in one swift motion. Then he looked at me, almost mournfully, cocking his head to the side. "You have to go."

I guffawed incredulously, "You can't be serious."

"Yes," he assured, his old, cocky, self returning. "You have to. I have to think, and I cannot fucking think with you here."

He dove on top of me over the covers. He nuzzled my neck, kissing me, and I felt my body snap back to attention. Every nerve ending crying out for more.

"I can't believe you would love me and leave me," I mocked, pushing his muscular chest, even though I wanted to pull him to me, pull him back inside me. He jumped up again and grabbed my clothes. My leggings, turtleneck sweater, and undergarments were all located in different spots on the floor. He handed the articles of clothing to me. I slid the turtleneck on over my head, still in bed under the comforter, before sliding my legs out of the bed and pulling my leggings on. I stood, and he looked me up and down.

"Fuck it," he uttered. And then he was on me again.

The interior lights were on in my car when I pulled down the visor and looked at myself in the mirror. I looked insane. Disheveled. My hair was a tangled mess, and my lips were red and swollen from what felt like, what could have been, literally hours of kissing. I started the engine, turned off the interior light, and put my car in gear. I cracked the windows and let the cold air whip around me as I made my way back to Culpepper Manor. Flashes of my night with Harrison entered my head as I drove, my insides involuntarily contracting at the memories.

I slipped into Culpepper Manor and tiptoed up the stairs. It was quiet and still, and I knew Theo and Tara had likely been asleep for a couple of hours. In my room, I slipped into my wingback chair by the fireplace and stared at nothing. My mind blank for the first time in a long time. A sort of meditation. Eventually, my mind drifted to the key. The little gold key I threw out of the window. *If I am meant to know, may the key come back to me,* I had uttered. A sign. Permission. Permission to know my family's fucked-up history, my mother's fucked-up history. I walked to my balcony, slid out of the door, and into the cold night air. I looked out, leaning over the banister, studying the ground and forest beyond. I pictured the key laying in the grass in the woods. Then I pictured it resting on a leaf. Then, I pictured the tiny gold object in a squirrel's belly, like Jonah and the whale.

I was shivering so hard my teeth were chattering when I found my way back inside to the warmth of my room. I sat back in my wingback chair and picked up the old spell book perched on my end table, Edith

Daisy's spell book, and flipped through to find the locator spell.

What is lost shall be found,

May my feet find the ground,

Where the object lay,

Time right away,

Eyes open wide,

What is lost shall no longer hide,

So mote it be.

I said the spell again and again, visualizing the tiny gold key. Visualizing the feel of the key in my palm, and visualizing my joy at having it returned to me. Repeating. Repeating. Repeating. Again and again and again, until I fell asleep in the chair.

My eyes shot open. I heard something. At first, I thought I had been dreaming, but then, no, I heard something. I recalled the murmuring and the chanting Harrison described, coming from the woods. I was so still; I could hear my heart pounding in the darkness—and the noise. *But what's that sound?* The sound wasn't murmuring or chanting. I stood from my chair and quietly slipped back out onto my balcony. It was freezing outside, and my feet and hands turned to ice instantly. My heart started pounding harder as I identified the noise: the familiar sound of a car coming up the winding drive in front of the house.

"Shit," I muttered, hurrying back inside my room, wondering if I had locked the front door. I darted out of my room and down the stairs, making my way into the foyer. I peeked out of one of the small, beveled glass windows next to the heavy wooden front door and, sure enough, a car—or more accurately a truck—was creeping down the driveway, headlights off. I sprinted back upstairs towards our sleeping quarters. "Someone's here!" I cried, not bothering to keep my voice down, flinging each of their doors open. "Someone's here!"

Theo and Tara were out in the hallway now, looking alarmed. I took a deep breath. "Someone in a truck is coming down the driveway. Their headlights are off."

"Don't turn on any lights!" Theo commanded, snapping into action. The three of us, all clad in our pajamas, all crept down the old stairs to the main foyer, towards the front door, in the dark. Fear rose in my throat; I felt like the villagers were coming with pitchforks.

"It's all the way up the driveway now," Tara whispered, moving towards one of the small, beveled windows, shifting her body slightly to get a better look beyond the stone portico, into the driveway. "So, it's not like a person just turning around."

"What should we do?" My voice was calmer now that I saw that I did, indeed, lock the front door. I moved in front of the heavy mahogany door, a human shield, standing on my tiptoes to peer out another of the small windows beside the frame.

"I'm calling the police," Theo announced, picking up what would now be considered an ancient landline, attached to a wooden paneled wall, and dialing. All of our cellphones were left upstairs in the panic, probably all still plugged in, charging for the night.

"I can almost make out the license plate," Tara relayed from the window, "It looks like maybe S15... I can't quite see the rest... It's too dark."

"The make and model of the car," Theo inquired.

"It looks to be a black truck. Maybe a Ford F-150..." Tara answered.

Theo was on the phone with the police now. I heard her relaying the information Tara had told her.

"Oh my gosh... someone's getting out of the truck!" Tara cried, in a hushed voice.

Through the small window, I could make out a vague figure, large, male, walking towards the portico. The silhouette slightly distorted from the antique beveling. Fear seized my entire body, and I felt temporarily paralyzed, my breath catching. But then something about the body size and gait looked vaguely familiar. Large, athletic, muscular, like a football player.

"Is that Cliff? Cliff Bishop?" I whispered.

"Oh my God, I'm pretty sure that is Cliff," Tara affirmed, sounding more annoyed now than scared.

"What should I do?" I asked.

"Just stay where you are. Both of you," Theo commanded. "The police are on their way. We don't know if that is Cliff for sure, and either way, it's best not to confront him."

I heard the mailbox, a fixture added when I was a child, open and then close, metal clanging on metal.

"He's putting something in the mailbox," I whispered. And then I saw his eyes through the window beside the door frame. I was staring out the window at him, as he was staring at me from the outside.

"Fuck!" I heard him yell, stumbling back. Then the sound of him falling on the stone.

"He fell," Tara laughed, her voice still in a hushed tone.

"That's definitely Cliff," I confirmed, calm now. Also annoyed now. And maybe annoyed was not the word. Furious seemed more accurate. *Mother fucker*.

I watched him stand and dust himself off, and then I slid away from the window where he could no longer see me.

"He's headed back to his truck. Oh my gosh, he is running!" Tara narrated. "Okay, he's leaving."

I listened as Theo related all of this to the operator, including Cliff's name. As if on cue, sirens sounded in the distance.

Travis Hodge stood in our sitting room, in his uniform, a ballpoint pen and a small pad in hand. "Okay, so he didn't try to break in?" he asked again.

"No," we all answered, again, in unison.

"Treasure heard him coming down the driveway and woke us up. We ran down here and watched him from the window while he stood on the portico. He put a note in our mailbox," she held up the note we snagged from the mailbox as soon as Cliff's truck left the driveway. "The note says: 'Leave town! We all know your family will face eternity in Hell's fire! You killed Jasper, and you killed Jenna!'"

Travis looked genuinely horrified, "Jesus Christ. Let me see the note." Tara handed him the note, and Travis took a photo with his phone.

"Go arrest him, Travis!" Tara demanded, her hands jutting out in an exasperated expression. "He trespassed on our property and threatened us!"

"He's been stopped," Travis assured us, looking at Tara sympathetically. "I heard it on the radio right before I knocked on your door. He's being booked right now, but on suspicion of DUI charges. It seems like he had one hell of a night, before he decided to make his way over here. If you all want to press charges against him, that is your right. I'll take down some information now, and we can file in the morning."

"We want to file charges!" Tara exclaimed. "This is absolutely ridiculous!"

"We received another threatening letter a few days ago," Theo interjected. "I reported it and gave it over to Chief Dodd. That letter was stuck on The Alchemist's door. Now, I am assuming it was also from Cliff?"

"Could be," Travis admitted. "Of course, it might be difficult to prove. But either way, he is very obviously harassing all of you. I'm really sorry about that."

Tara crossed her arms, obviously not wanting to be consoled. She wanted action. Hell, we all wanted action. Cliff had been a thorn in our side for the better part of a year now. "Can you all do something about it then? Please!"

"Listen, we will do everything we can," he responded.

"Thank you so much, officer," Theo said graciously.

Tara snorted, her eyes rolling up into her head.

"Look," Travis said, looking at Tara and then the rest of us. "I know it's been rough for the three of you. I'm going to do everything I can, along with Chief Dodd, to make it better." He smiled ruefully then, the Travis from our childhood shining through, despite his uniform and professional demeanor. "And… if it makes you guys feel any better… when one of our guys pulled Cliff over…" he paused again for dramatic effect, "They realized he had pissed his pants."

We made a spot at the kitchen table. "Could you imagine if Travis had come in here?" Tara cackled, moving each item carefully so we each had a spot. "Just spell books, grimoires, and other witch paraphernalia all over the place."

"Maybe he would have pissed his pants too," I remarked, and we all laughed.

"I can't believe he pissed his pants!" Tara howled, laughing so hard she was holding her stomach.

I sat at the table in a spot that Tara had cleared. Tara slumped into a chair next to me. Theo was rummaging through the fridge. "We need snacks!" was all she said, as she put some of Deidra's homemade doughnuts on the table. I reached for a glazed apple fritter and pulled a large piece off. I felt suddenly ravenous, like I hadn't eaten in years.

"Treasure scared the shit out of him!" Tara bellowed. "I didn't think you had it in you!"

"Well, to be honest," I confessed. "I didn't do it on purpose. I just happened to be looking out when he looked in."

"He must have pissed himself when he saw you in the window!"

"Imagine pulling up to a 'witch house,'" Theo said, putting 'witch house' in air quotes with her fingers, "Looking into the window and seeing two eyes peering back at you!"

Tara burst into another fit of laughter, "I will never forget this!"

"Oh man!" Theo exclaimed. "What a night!"

"I'm sure they will somehow make this our fault, you know, Cliff getting arrested... again," I said darkly, somewhat spoiling the light mood.

Theo nodded, "I'm sure. Like we have nothing better to do than follow Cliff around and try to get him in trouble."

"Can't really blame us for the drinking and driving though," Tara commented.

"Oh, I'm sure we'll get another note," I joked and then switched to a stereotypical witchy voice, "I know you made Cliff drink. You're the reason he's a belligerent, daft, asshole."

"With pee pants," Tara added, and we all cracked up.

I sighed heavily, "So, I have to tell you guys. I tried a spell."

Both Theo and Tara sat up straighter. "What kind of spell?" Theo inquired, jutting her chin towards me.

"A locator spell... for the gold key. One of the books I have belonged to this woman... Edith Daisy... I don't know if that rings a bell for anyone," I began. Both Theo and Tara shook their heads no. "She has tons and tons of spells in the book. And I thought I would try it."

"Is that what you were doing at Deidra's?" Tara asked, now picking at a maple-frosted crème-filled long john.

"No," I responded, recalling my night with Harrison. And my lie. "I did it when I got home."

"So, what happens now?" Tara looked earnest. She was far more engaged in this topic than I expected her to be.

"I guess I wait? I don't know."

"Spells usually require action," Theo explained. "You don't just do the spell but do the action. Go look for it. Concentrate. See if you can find it."

I nodded in agreement. "Okay, I will first thing tomorrow morning."

"There's not a whole lot that I would consider interesting in what I'm reading so far. It's someone's day-to-day journal. Someone boring. Haven't found a name yet," Tara explained.

We looked at Theo, who was currently looking quite sick. "Theo?" I asked. "Have you been going through any of the stuff?"

"Well, I wasn't sure how to tell you guys this, but I've been reading one of Mom's journals.... And I came across Chief Dodd's name... in a romantic capacity."

"What?!" I exhaled, the word coming out with breath. "What do you mean?"

"I mean, it sounds like... and you guys can read it... Mom was having a fling with Dodd."

I looked over at Tara seated next to me. Her face had gone white, and she had tears in her eyes.

"Tara, what's wrong?" I grabbed her arm and pulled her into me.

"No... no... don't do that," she begged, "I'll cry." But she was already crying.

Theo leapt up from her chair and went over to her.

"What's wrong?" Theo cooed, rubbing Tara's head, patting her hair down.

"I never told you guys this but... Do you remember Jasper's mom?"

I did. Horrible old woman. Seemingly ancient, even when we were quite young. As children, we would see her from time to time around Seven Hills. When she would spot us or our mother, she would bolt, even before Jasper disappeared. She would make scenes, trying to get away from us. And we were *technically* her grandchildren. We *were* her grandchildren. The grandchildren she never wanted and clearly highly disapproved of. I didn't know much about Jasper and his family, his parents. But I knew they hated my mother and Aunt Elaina, and us—by extension.

As far as I knew, the old woman still lived in Seven Hills, in one of the grandest homes in town, in the historic district, not far from the now-empty VanHoy estate. I hadn't seen her in years and years.

In fact, I couldn't remember the last time. It was very possible she was no longer alive.

"Well..." Tara continued, "I saw her once, and she approached me. Just came right up to me and said, 'You're not Jasper's. Who knows who your daddy is.'" Tara was softly crying now, tears streaming from her eyes. "It's why I left. I couldn't deal with this place anymore."

I remembered when Tara left. During that time, she seemed to have lived all over the place, even briefly in Europe. We would get random postcards, but other than that, we rarely heard from her. And then she just came home. No explanation given.

A thought occurred to me, and I cleared my throat. "Who cares who your dad is? None of us have a dad."

"Do you think it's possible Chief Dodd..." Tara's voice trailed off, and she wiped her tears with the back of her shirt sleeve.

"Is your father?" Theo finished her sentence. "I mean I don't think so. I guess it's not impossible. I can look for a year in the journal. But..."

"It would almost be a relief if Chief Dodd *was* your dad. At least it means you wouldn't be related to Jasper and his nightmare of a mother," I pointed out, trying to make Tara laugh, but she didn't so much as smile.

"Sometimes, I feel like I hate Mom," she admitted, beginning to cry again. "Because she just couldn't be normal. She just couldn't. Not for our sake and not for her sake. She couldn't just try to fit in, be like the other moms. I just feel so angry. So angry *at her*. And then she just died and left us here."

Theo nodded sympathetically, tears in her eyes. I think we had all wished we could be normal at some point or another, all wished our mother, our family, could be normal. Silence passed between us, and I was wiping away my own tears now.

"Mom couldn't be normal," Theo tried to explain. "Because she was so spectacular. She was magical."

My eyes shot open for the second time tonight, and I was wide awake, lying in bed. I laid still. Another noise. A loud rustling. A soft, high-pitched cry. First, I thought of Jenna, lost in the woods, searching for her family, running through the trees when she spotted a house. Our house. Culpepper Manor. But I knew that it was likely not Jenna. I knew, as the days passed, Jenna would likely not be found. At least not in the way we would like her to be. Then, I thought maybe Cliff had returned. *Maybe they had released him from the drunk tank, and he came back to enact his revenge? Or, perhaps, this time, he sent others?*

I got out of bed and checked my phone: 5 am. A few hours had passed since Theo, Tara, and I packed away our snacks and went to bed, exhausted from the night's events. This time, I threw on a warm robe and some fuzzy slippers before slipping out onto my balcony. I watched my breath as I exhaled. There was rustling coming from below. I peered down to the ground where yellow eyes stared back up at me, and I flinched, taking a step back. Just a cat. A black cat, mewing so loudly it woke me up. I stared at the cat, entranced, pacing back and forth. Occasionally baring its teeth up at me, mouth open in a cat's, sharp, cry. And then, something else caught my eye, glinting in the moonlight. Shining. The cat circled.

I walked downstairs to the foyer, and then out of the front door. I walked around the house until I was underneath my balcony. I walked slowly towards the cat, which I had expected to become alarmed at my presence and flee. But it didn't. It continued its odd behavior. I slowed my pace, making a clicking noise with my tongue, and the cat stopped. It mewed at me. I could see its sharp teeth glinting like polished ivory in the moonlight. I continued to walk closer and closer to the animal until, there in the grass, I saw it. The gold key.

Chapter 7

Today is Ostara. Today we celebrate the Spring Equinox. Ostara is a time to celebrate rebirth, after winter strips the world bare. Now, we plant the seeds that will become our future, just as we plant the literal seeds that will become our lifeline the following year. We do this just as our ancestors did for generations and generations before them. One long line, dating all the way back to the beginning of humanity.

"Happy Ostara!" Theo bellowed, as we all stood in the kitchen in the early morning, drinking coffee from our seldom-used coffee maker. *Why make coffee at home, when you can get the most delicious hot coffee from Seven Sweets?* This has somewhat been the Culpepper family moto ever since Deidra opened her bakery. After the events of last night, however, we all needed extra fuel before making our way out into the world.

"Happy Ostara," Tara and I groaned in unison.

"What is one 'seed' you are all hoping to plant today?" Theo asked brightly, tying a work apron around her waist.

Tara and I looked at each other, feeling almost too tired to play along, but knowing this was the very least we could do for Theo, who loved tradition above all else.

"I'm planting a seed that will turn into a buff man with arms the size of watermelons," Tara declared, after taking a swig from her hot pink coffee mug. "And a pen—"

"Okay, thanks. Treasure?" Theo asked me, cutting off Tara.

I considered this. "Hmmm," I began, taking a sip of inferior hot coffee from my own mug. "I'm planting the seeds of self-discovery. Of turning into the person I want to be."

Now Tara was rolling her eyes. "Can we go now?" is all she asked.

"Yes," Theo responded.

But we all stood around for a few more minutes, finishing our hot coffee in slow gulps, until we began the long process of loading our vehicles with everything we needed for the festival.

The air was cold outside, but the sort of cold that promised to warm up into a beautiful, almost spring-like day. It was the sort of day you began with a jacket and gloves but abandoned around midday. The sky was a bright crystal blue, and the sun was shining. It was the perfect day for the Ostara Festival. We arrived downtown, where we parked on the street to haul in all of our items. The worst part of the festival was all the time it took to take every item over to your booth. We would also have to make a trip to The Alchemist to pick up our giant hare and pastel-colored egg for our booth decorations. I began the day exhausted, and I was already dreading lugging the wooden objects through town. *We need someone with a truck*, I thought, and Cliff's Ford F-150 popped into my head. Maybe he would help load up everything we needed if we promised to discontinue our killing spree and keep the whole pissing-the-pants thing "hush hush." I smiled.

We began setting up our table booth, arranging our cleaning supplies, spring candles, homemade bundles, crystals, and more for people to browse. We shoved the boxes with extra product underneath the table, which would be hidden by a tablecloth with a large brown bunny on it that Theo had bought years ago. "It's vintage!" she had exclaimed when she brought it home, showing us the brown bunny. Unfortunately, and as usual, neither Tara nor I matched her enthusiasm. But looking at the booth, I had to admit, it was a nice touch. The large hare and the egg flanked our table, making our booth stand out from all the others.

"Happy Ostara!" Deidra called, as she approached our booth, a beverage carrier filled with four coffees in hand.

"Happy Ostara!" We yelled back, all grateful to see Seven Sweets coffee—and Deidra, of course.

"I'm setting up next to you all," Deidra announced. Deidra was decked out in a gray hoodie with an iron-on Easter bunny. "We can't eat all the treats right away. We have to save some for customers. Or, at the very least, that is what I am supposed to say as a business owner." She winked at us.

I laughed and then asked, "What do you have this year?" I couldn't help myself.

"This year, we did homemade Rice Krispie treats with pastel M&Ms, lemon-blueberry poppy-seed bread, egg-shaped cut-out cookies, lavender macarons, mini strawberry shortcakes, chocolate marshmallow cookies, meringue cookies... oh and... blondies!"

"Oh my gosh. That sounds amazing!" I said, my stomach rumbling. *I have to get on a consistent meal schedule,* I thought.

"Do you have eggs for the hunt?" Theo asked Deidra. "If you do, I can take the box to the pavilion. They have a group of high schoolers that are going to hide them in the square for the kids." *It's always nice that Theo knows what is going on*, I thought. I have been so caught up in Jenna's disappearance, Cliff's threats, what we found in the attic, the gold key, and... well... Harrison... that I had no idea what the schedule was, who was running the show, or where everything went.

"Yes," Deidra responded. "I'll let Maria know. She is bringing the box up from Seven Sweets." Maria was a long-time employee at Seven Sweets and had become a sort of right-hand for Deidra. "She also offered to staff your booth while we all go to lunch. I'll have plenty of people in and out to run mine."

I put an arm around Deidra's shoulders and squeezed. "I'm just so proud of you!" I exclaimed. "Look at everything you've done!"

Deidra smiled and slipped her arm around my waist. "Plus, we need to catch up today! I feel like I haven't seen you!"

Tara's head popped up from where she was looking down at our booth, rearranging items. "Wasn't she with you last night?" she demanded.

Shit.

"Well, there is always more to catch up on," I responded lightly, and squeezed Deidra's shoulders a little tighter. I could feel both Tara and Deidra give me strange looks, but it was true, at least to some extent. A lot happened last night.

"Happy Ostara!" I cheered.

Tara was like a bloodhound when she smelled bullshit. I felt lucky the morning was so busy that she barely had time to question me. I also felt happy that our items, especially our cleaning products, were selling like hotcakes. At this point, we might sell out of everything, even our inventory on the shelves in our store, before we packed it in for the day. I also realized that I felt normal, happy even. For the first time, in what felt like a long time, I felt truly hopeful. It felt like a good day to "start over." Begin again.

The Magician

"Okay, the egg hunt is underway!" Theo declared, as she stood from her chair at our booth. We all stood to watch the egg hunt. Children, mostly all under 12, dressed in brightly colored jackets and mittens, raced, carrying pastel-colored baskets, to find all the eggs in the downtown square. Parents were helping the very little ones, as all the children found eggs in the pavilion, on the lawn, on tree branches, next to rocks, and even near the bottom of some booths. Many of the children held their eggs up in triumph as each one was found. We all clapped.

"So… Treasure…" Tara began, taking advantage of the lack of customers as we all watched the egg hunt.

"Hold on," I replied, before she could get more out. "I'm going to get a cookie from Deidra."

I inelegantly left our booth to stand behind the Seven Sweets booth, on the opposite side of Deidra.

"More cookies?" Deidra offered, as she clapped her hands for a child that just found a pale-yellow egg in a neatly trimmed hedge. "Good find!" she yelled, giving him a thumbs-up.

"Yes," I said. "We are definitely going to need more."

"So, why'd you lie?" she asked, but she was smiling slyly. "You could have filled me in at least!"

I laughed. "I promise, I will! It really has been crazy. Actually, there is a lot to fill you in on…"

I felt his presence before I saw him, almost like I could sense his energy. I scanned the crowd and saw his face. Harrison was approaching the Seven Sweets booth looking like a GQ model ripped straight from a magazine. The background seemed to blur, and, for a moment, it was only him I saw. He was wearing his "detective" clothes now: dress pants and a navy-blue button-down dress shirt with a jacket. Each item of clothing fit him like it was made for him. What he lacked in home décor; he made up for in wardrobe. I could feel my face heat up, thinking of my night with him at his apartment.

"Oh my God, Detective Harrison is coming this way!" Deidra whispered urgently, trying to move her lips as little as possible. She nudged me with her elbow, as if to say, "act natural."

"Ladies," Harrison greeted, when he was close enough for us to hear, and gave us all a slight bow. "Booths are looking great."

"Thank you," Deidra responded. "Can I interest you in a spring treat?"

"No, thank you," he replied. "But I did stop by Seven Sweets earlier for a cup of coffee. Miss Culpepper and Miss Culpepper." He nodded at both Theo and Tara, who looked at him somewhat mystified, and I wondered if they were also somewhat entranced by his appearance.

Once he was closer, he turned to look at me, made eye contact, and uttered a third, "Miss Culpepper," with a slight smile and a nod of his head. Then, he came to stand next to me, shoulder to shoulder, looking out on the spectacle that was the egg hunt, that was Seven Hills and its traditions.

"Great turnout," Deidra commented, making polite conversation. Deidra never was one for long stretches of silence.

"Seems that way," Harrison responded politely.

"Is this your first Ostara Festival?" Deidra asked, leaning forward slightly to look past me to Harrison.

"The very first," he stated with a grin.

And then I felt his fingers, down by his side, stroke mine, also positioned at my side. The lightest and most delicate of touches.

"Well, I hope you enjoy. As much as you can, of course," she replied.

He captured my pinky finger between his thumb and pointer finger and caressed, and I was landed immobile, looking straight ahead, a neutral expression on my face. Electricity traveled through my body, my stomach squeezed, but I did my best to not betray anything on my face. *I am an immovable statue*, I told myself.

"That is very kind of you," he responded, with another toothy grin. "Well ladies, I am just passing through. I had better be going."

"Of course," Deidra affirmed, warmly. "You probably have a lot on your plate."

He weaved his fingers through mine, gently stroking down each of my fingers with his. Again, words from my mother's diary flashed in my mind, *I am a goner now*.

"Yes, I do. And with that, I will have to bid you ladies adieu. Happy Ostara."

"Thank you so much," Deidra replied.

Harrison released my hand, turned, and gave us a stunning, almost devilish grin, and walked back into the crowd.

"Oh my God, Treasure," Deidra started, turning towards me, looking at me, studying my face. At first, I thought she had found us out. She was going to accuse us of being together, but instead she just said, "You were being so rude!"

I ordered a giant chicken Caesar salad, with extra chicken, from Boil and Broom, a relatively new and trendy restaurant in town, down the street from The Alchemist. Maria graciously offered to watch The Alchemist's booth while Deidra, Theo, Tara, and I went out for lunch. Hannah, another one of Deidra's employees, was staffing the Seven Sweets table in her absence.

"I'm not sure what Treasure filled you in on," Theo said to Deidra, not long after we had ordered our food. "So much has happened in the last few days." Theo began, telling Deidra everything—in detail. First, she explained the keys Tara and I found, the items in the attic, her memories of Mom and Aunt Elaina taking books up there after Jasper's disappearance, although she had not made the connection between the two events at that time. She described the Mason jar, and Ronnie's assessment of the item, checking in with me to verify the accuracy in her retelling.

All three of us, the Culpepper women, worked in tandem to explain what we found in the journals. Theo explained what she had read about our mother and Chief Dodd. To all of our surprise, Tara even shared with Deidra what Jasper's mom had said to her, the questions surrounding her paternity. She stated how it made her feel, and why she decided to leave town years and years ago. Deidra reached across the table and held Tara's small hand at this admission. We all had tears rimming our eyes. Theo dabbed at the corners of her own eyes with a cloth napkin from the table. I did the same before uttering, "We are all such babies!"

I explained what I read about my mother's and Jasper's relationship, detailing the bruised wrist, the self-described obsession. Then, I described my horror at this information, my decision to throw the tiny gold key out of the window, and then to use Edith Daisy's spell book to try to retrieve it.

"Last night," I explained to everyone. "I woke up to a noise. The second wake-up to a noise. We will tell you about the first one in a minute. I looked outside and, in the moonlight, I could see the key sparkling. I found it... or maybe more accurately... it came back to me."

All three women looked completely stunned.

"That is incredible!" Theo exclaimed, clasping her hands together, delighted. "Just incredible."

"It might have been the most surreal moment of my life," I admitted, remembering the feeling of seeing the key glinting in the moonlight. "I've never experienced anything like it... and also... I haven't said this out loud yet... but... I've been thinking about the Mason jar... and the apparition in my room. So, as you all know at least Ronnie thinks, the Mason jar might have been a binding or banishing spell.... You literally put someone on ice... in water.... And well... that apparition in my room, a male, was dripping on my floor. Do you think whoever they put in that Mason jar, so to speak, was also in my room?"

"Holy shit," Tara blurted, pausing with her fork in midair. "I didn't think about that."

"The hairs on the back of my neck are standing up right now," Deidra declared, crossing her arms and rubbing each of them with her hands.

"Me too," Theo agreed.

As if saving the best for last, we all took turns explaining parts of the Cliff story. We laid out the details of the threatening letters, the window, the loud thump, and last, but certainly not least, Travis telling us about Cliff peeing his pants. We all laughed heartily at this, between taking bites of our respective meals that had arrived at some point during the storytelling session.

"We have to go into the police station to formally fill out all the paperwork," Theo explained. "To press charges. But in the light of day... I am almost wondering if this would be a waste of time and resources. I mean, there is a missing girl out there. Besides, what are they really going to do? He came to the house and dropped something off. It wasn't even an outright threat."

Tara nodded, but added, "Yea... but I still want his ass to fry."

We all laughed.

Deidra looked solemn then. "The press conference for Jenna is tonight. It's going to be held at the church in town. Then, there is going to be another candlelight vigil—this time at the high school football field. Are you guys going to go?"

The three of us exchanged glances, and I spoke up first. "I honestly don't think it would be a good idea for us to go. I think any sane person would not suspect we are involved with this in any way, but there seems to be so many insane people around here."

Theo nodded. "Let's just support from afar," she paused. "Five days gone. It's so scary. I don't know if they are ever going to find her."

We were all silent, feeling the weight of Theo's words. We were all thinking it, but she was the first to say the quiet part aloud. The hopeful feeling of the day seemed to deflate a bit. A young woman, before her life had even really started, was gone. Nowhere to be found.

"Okay," Deidra said with some resolve. "Let's try to just get out there and enjoy the rest of this beautiful day. Spring is coming! Besides, we can only do what we can do. I will be there tonight in support, representing all four of us."

We all got up and stood in line to pay our checks, all of us a little more solemn then when we arrived.

"Oh, and there is one more thing I forgot to mention," I added, as we are exiting the restaurant, wanting the pleasant mood from before to return. "We have a cat now."

When we arrived back to the town square, it was significantly less busy than before. It seemed most of the easter egg "hunters," and many of their parents, had dissipated. We relieved Maria and Hannah so that they could go procure their own lunch.

"Now, we can just chill out and enjoy the beautiful weather," Deidra stated, as we resumed our spots behind our booths.

"Hello," a male voice called from behind us. All four of us turned around to see Cliff Bishop. He was dressed in a pair of light-colored jeans and a red, plaid jacket. He looked angry; his face almost as red as the jacket.

"Get out of here Cliff," Tara started, and Theo put a hand on her arm, warning her to not get into it with him.

"I have just as much right to be here as anyone else," he argued, crossing his large arms defiantly.

"Yes, but you certainly do not have the right to be on our property," I declared, making my lips into one long line and cocking my head. Theo's warnings be damned.

He stood up straighter. "You can't prove shit. And even if you have some sort of 'ring cam,' all I did was drop off a note. And you baby-killers are lucky that's all I did."

"That's a threat, Cliff," Theo scolded, raising her voice a bit. "And I think we might have to share that with the police."

"Why do you all continue to give me problems? You keep the police out of this," he warned, gruffly, pointing his finger at Theo. "I know you witches are involved in some way. I've seen the proof, the stuff in her car…"

"What the hell are you talking about Cliff? What stuff in her car?" Tara demanded angrily.

"Stuff from The Alchemist. What'd you do with her? Is this all a coincidence? So, you're telling me…" He paused, rubbing his chin, a grim smile on his face. "Your father, who I hear was causing your Mama nothing but troubles… disappears. And you all had nothing to do with it. Then, VanHoy, who I hear was causing you all nothing but troubles also 'disappears,' bashed over the head…. And don't try to tell me you all weren't involved with his murdering wife. I hear things. People have seen you all together. At your Satan shop, doing God knows what. And then lastly, here's me, minding my own business, but I guess I cause you all problems and then—poof—my cousin disappears. And… what'd you know? Her car is found on your property… with shit from your God-forsaken store in the glove box. Believe me when I say others in town might be blind to your shit, but trust me when I say I am not!" We all looked at each other with matching expressions of horror, too stunned to speak. Cliff continued, "I'm just going to say this once more. Watch your fucking back. It would be for the best if you all would just leave town."

Cliff turned, back hunched, and walked away like a man possessed. I never knew that someone's gait could look angry, furious. So, Cliff, and likely his family, really did and still think we were involved with Jenna's disappearance. That we stole his cousin to get back at him. To ruin him.

Deidra's hand was at her throat when she gasped, "I'm scared. I think maybe you all should call the police."

"Maybe we honestly should leave town," Tara said, her own pretty face beat red with suppressed anger. "I really don't know how much more of this I can take."

"Let's pack it in and go home for the day. Stay out of the way. Lie low for a while. We had a great day of sales, let's just go home where we know we will be safe," Theo offered.

"But he's already been out to Culpepper Manor. How do we know we will be safe there?" I lamented, looking at each one of them.

"You can all stay at my place," Deidra offered. "I know I don't have much room, but I have the pull-out couch and an air mattress…"

"No," Theo avowed, figuratively putting her foot down. "We don't leave Culpepper Manor. Not now and not ever. Like all the women before us, we don't cow tail to this shit." I looked at the shocked expressions on Deidra and Tara's faces. They'd never seen Theo this angry and neither had I. But she was right. I thought of Sarah Culpepper and the cow's tongue. Sarah Culpepper did the almost impossible: she beat a Witchcraft charge in a time where women had virtually no rights. Mom and Aunt Elaina, at least we could assume, also did what they needed to do to protect their family. We have evidence they bound their enemies. These women would not sit idly by.

"No, we don't," I agreed. "Like Sarah Culpepper, like Mom, like Aunt Elaina. We do what we can do—what is our birthright.… We use Magick."

We all, indeed, packed it in and went back to Culpepper Manor. The three of us in our respective vehicles and Deidra in hers—one long processional back to our estate. Deidra insisted she come back with us to stay. When we arrived home, I ran up the stairs to my room to retrieve Edith Daisy's spell book. I flipped through the fragile book until I found the protection spell.

"We have to do this right," Theo stipulated, taking the spell book from me. "I hope I remember how to do everything correctly. We need salt, water, and maybe some chalk. We have to cast a proper circle."

"What should I do?" Deidra asked, looking rather overwhelmed.

"You're going to help us," I informed her, and she then looked a bit nervous. "We need you to help us." I took her hand, reassuring her: It would all be alright.

The four of us spent a couple of hours completely washing down a room in the seldom used, let alone entered, servant's quarters with salt water, all of our arms aching by the end of the task. While it was still chilly outside, the four of us were now sweating, each of us having shed our layers in the process. By the time we were completely finished scrubbing the entire room, including the ceiling, the sun had gone down.

"Now, we have to cast a circle," Theo explained, drawing a large pentagram in a circle on the wooden floor. "We will need everything and everyone in the circle. Once we cast it, we cannot break it until we are done. We are going to need candles, matches, salt in a bowl, selenite, a small black cloth, and the spell book. Oh... and there is one more thing... a lot of times it's better to practice... skyclad."

"Skyclad?" Deidra asked, a look of confusion on her face.

"Um... yes, skyclad means... nude," Theo explained, an apologetic look on her face. "Clothes can sometimes inhibit the energy moving from us to where it needs to go... if that makes sense."

"Oh my gosh! Are you serious?" Deidra cried, looking at all of us as if we were Martians.

"We totally understand if you don't feel comfortable with that!" I declared. "You absolutely do not have to do it."

Deidra laughed at the sincerity of my words. "Okay, if we're gonna do it, let's just do it. I just wish I had laid off the meringue cookies before this."

We all laughed and then scattered across Culpepper Manor to find the items we needed. Once we had gathered everything, we, one by one, placed it all neatly in a circle, a candle at each point of the pentagram. Theo also grabbed a photo of our mother and Aunt Elaina to place in the circle. We entered the circle.

"Throw your clothes out," Theo demanded. "We are going to cast the circle now."

We each undressed and threw our clothes into a corner outside of the circle. Three times we walked inside the circle, chanting, a message to the Gods and Goddesses of our intentions, a message to the evil spirits and negative energies to leave us. Negativity of any kind was banned from the circle.

"Now, we meditate," Theo instructed. And then proclaimed to the Gods and Goddesses, to the Universe, "And if it harm none, do what ye will."

Standing at an equal distance around the circle, we closed our eyes and concentrated. When I closed my eyes, I saw a spring day, a blue sky, large fluffy white clouds floating as far as I could see. I was with my sisters—all of my sisters—biological, chosen, generational, and even those I had not met and would likely never meet. I felt their presences so profoundly, a tear slipped down my cheek. I silently invited them into our circle, and I felt a love so intense that I began to sob. Inside my body, I could feel all my veins, like roots, coming alive, spreading down into the floor, under the floorboards, into the earth, moving to connect me with all things.

Time slipped by. It could have been five minutes or an hour when Theo finally spoke. I opened my eyes to see her flipping through Edith Daisy's spell book.

"We need protection. There are people that wish us harm," she paused to read the spell:

By the wind and by the fire,

Grant us the protection that we desire.

Stand by our side, a silent guard.

Do not allow Cliff Bishop to do us harm.

So mote it be.

Theo spoke the words, the spell, again and again, until we all joined in, chanting in unison. Our voices one rhythmic sound. I continued to chant but closed my eyes. When I closed my eyes, I saw the Seven Hills Cemetery. But now, in the cemetery, there was just one lone tombstone that read, *Diana Culpepper: A Beautiful Mother*. Nothing else but grass and blue sky for miles. No puffy clouds. An alternate universe.

Then Cliff came slamming into my mind, my meditation. I saw him threatening us. I saw him shouting. I saw him grab Sarah Tarleton's wrist, just as my father, Jasper, grabbed my mother's beautiful wrist. I watched this again and again. Until I wasn't sure if I was seeing Jasper or Cliff. I was not sure who was who. I felt dizzy, and my ears throbbed until they popped and started ringing. Tears slid down my face, and I didn't know if others could hear me crying. In fact, I didn't know if I was crying. Or screaming. Then I got a feeling so distinct, so real, that it might as well have been a message whispered into my ear. Cliff means to do us harm and *is willing* to do us harm. *There is not only bark, there is bite*, my gut screamed at me. Then, I could see into his body, into his core, and it was rotten filth. A hollowed-out tree. I heard his threats again. I tried to search for something other than sheer anger, empathy for him, compassion maybe, something. Something other than rage. But then, all I saw was red.

I dreamt I was in the woods, the trees so thick you could not see past the ones in front of you. It was spring. Between the massive trunks, covered in thick green bark and moss, I saw movement. At first, I thought: *It's a deer.* I kept walking, looking over my left shoulder, tracking the animal's movements. Then, I knew it was not a deer. It was Harrison. I could see his bright blue eyes through the trees as we walked in a parallel line. Trees passed between us.

Then, we were running, keeping pace with one another, and I was trying to catch a glance at him, just one glance. I was covered in sweat. We were in a heat so oppressive, I could barely breathe. The forest was closing in on us. We were parallel, never to cross, no matter how far—or how fast I ran. I came to a clearing, and Harrison was gone.

There was a pentagram drawn in stark white chalk on the green, green grass. I was nude. I looked up to see who I instinctually knew was Sarah Culpepper, also nude, standing in the circle. She laughed when I looked at her and said, "And here I thought you would never come."

A noise woke me up, and, for a moment, I had no idea where I was. I sat up, gasping. I was in my room, in my own bed. I sat very still, listening. *Could it be Cliff again? Could he be back?* And then I realized the sound was my phone, vibrating on my bedside table. The time was 1:11 am. I looked at the screen and saw I had text messages from Harrison.

Harrison: Treasure

Harrison: I need pillows and blankets.

I smiled despite myself and began to type.

Me: You do.

Harrison: I thought you were going to bring me some.

Me: I will.

Harrison: Bring them now.

Me: It's 1 am.

Harrison: I'll make it worth your trouble.

Me: I'm listening.

Harrison: Come here, and I'll show you.

I knew before I even finished reading the last text message that I was, indeed, going.

I tiptoed downstairs to where Deidra was asleep in the makeshift bed we made for her on the couch. I shook her a little bit, extra blankets and pillows from my closet in hand.

"What are you doing?" she asked, groggily.

"I'm headed out," I told her.

"What? To where?" she questioned, sitting up, rubbing her eyes.

"I'm going to Harrison's apartment," I explained. "I'll send you a pin, so you know where I am."

"Why the hell are you going there?" she exclaimed, more awake now.

"I don't know…" my voice trailed off. "I guess we have like… a thing."

"Oh my gosh! Seriously? What do you mean 'a thing'?"

"I really don't know. But I'm gonna lock the door behind me. Go upstairs and sleep in my room. Lock the bedroom door too. I'm going to keep my phone by me. Call if you need me."

She laughed, "I want details in the morning! And I do mean very *detailed* details."

I snickered along with her: "Okay, I feel like it's the very least I can do."

I knocked on Harrison's door, which he opened, wearing a crisp, white t-shirt and grey sweatpants. He had slightly wet hair again. I shoved the blankets and pillows towards him, and he grinned broadly. He looked handsome, but I noticed that his eyes were bloodshot, and he looked incredibly tired.

"Are you going to let me in?" I asked, smiling at him, still standing in the doorway.

"Only if you promise to stay the entire night this time," he responded, taking the bedding.

"Last night, you were the one who asked me to leave! Something about 'you can't think' if I recall correctly," I jeered, trying to imitate his voice.

"Well, I don't wanna think at all tonight," he admitted, throwing the bedding on the floor in his apartment and grabbing my hands, intertwining our fingers. "I'm so over thinking, I might never think again."

And he was in my space, kissing my neck, kissing my lips, murmuring indistinct words between contact. Harrison's hands were everywhere all at once, in my hair, holding my face, up my shirt, down my pants, searching for moisture inside and dragging it up to the top of me. The term *root chakra* flashed through my mind, but I felt anything but grounded. I was flying, as he picked me up and took me to his bedroom, yellow flecks of light in the darkness behind my eyelids.

Chapter 8

There was banging, and for the second time, I awoke having no idea where I was. I rolled over to see Harrison's dark head of hair, his face smashed into his pillow, and remembered it all. The spell. His text. Driving over here in the early morning. Our night together.

"Detective Harrison," I said, my voice scratchy. I pushed myself up and onto my elbows, and then wiggled his muscular arm in an attempt to wake him.

He turned to me and opened his eyes, his face crisscrossed with lines from the pillow he was face down on moments before. Harrison was sleeping on a decorative, tufted pillow sham from Culpepper Manor… like an animal. I debated telling him you are supposed remove the sham to sleep—when he spoke.

"You are really still calling me Detective Harrison?" he mocked, tiredly, and laughed despite the abrupt wake-up. He reached his hand over and tangled it into my hair.

"Someone's banging on your door," I whispered, feeling a little uneasy in the darkness, in this foreign place.

"I think you were dreaming..." he began, but then the knock sounded again. "Oh shit." He sprang out of bed and put on his sweatpants—nothing underneath. "Hold on."

Harrison exited the bedroom and flipped on the light in the living room, the bedroom illuminating. He opened the door out into the apartment hallway, and I could hear Travis' voice.

"Detective Harrison," he began, sounding a bit nervous. "I am so sorry to wake you. But it's an emergency. We need all-hands-on-deck right now."

"Okay," Harrison said, impatiently. "What's going on?"

"Cliff Bishop just gave us a call, claims the three Culpepper girls were standing outside of his bedroom window. He says they were threatening him, maybe stalking him? I don't know. He's got a group of people all riled up, and now they are downtown looking to bust some shit up."

I jumped up and threw Harrison's white t-shirt over my head and then pulled on my own pajama pants.

"What the hell?" I asked, arriving at the door next to Harrison. Travis looked startled and then shocked. Harrison looked down at me, a bit annoyed. "What did Cliff say?" I demanded.

"Treasure?" Travis shrieked in surprise. "What are you doing here? When did you get here?"

"Around 1:30-1:45 am," Harrison interjected, a bit protectively. I winced at what this sounded like,

The Magician

me slinking into his apartment at 1:30 am. "When did Cliff call this in?"

"About 20 minutes ago," Travis responded, looking at the watch on his wrist. "And its 4 am now. Shit. I knew he was lying."

"Let me get dressed," Harrison said, looking wide awake now.

"I'm going too," I announced. "What if they vandalize The Alchemist?"

"Okay hold on, hold on," Harrison commanded, his attention focused on me now.

Travis looked between us uncomfortably and stepped back out of the door. "I'll give you two a minute."

Harrison closed the door behind him, and then, again, turned to look at me. "You stay here. I'll go, check it out, and come back."

"But The Alchemist—" I began, but he cut me off.

"I'll take care of everything," he said, reassuringly, soothingly. "Let me take care of everything."

"Maybe I should go home. Theo and Tara..." I started again.

"Treasure. Treasure. Listen. This has the potential to get a little dangerous. Please let me go and assess the situation. Don't go home. Don't call your sisters right now. Let me see what's going on. Just stay here, and I promise to tell you everything that happens when I get back."

"Fine," I relented. "But hurry. Who knows what they will do."

He quickly changed into his "detective clothes" and headed out the door, instructing me to lock it behind him. I did, making sure to do the deadbolt.

I tried to sleep with no luck. Eventually, I ended up lying on Harrison's leather couch, the pillows and blankets from Culpepper Manor stacked on top of me. I flipped through the late-night reruns, pausing on one of my favorite *Golden Girls* episodes: the one where Rose shoots the vase. I let the episode "lull" me into a semi-calm state. At around 6:30 am, a knock sounded on the door.

"Treasure," a familiar voice sounded through the door, and I heard a key in the lock. I undid the deadbolt, allowing him back into his apartment. "You okay?" he asked me when he slipped inside.

"I don't know," I admitted. "What happened?" I wouldn't know if I was okay until I heard what happened at The Alchemist.

"There's some damage downtown," he relayed, tiredly. "But it's mostly trash and eggs thrown around. Most of the people had scattered by the time Travis and I got down there. Beyond that, there is no damage to your store. At least none that we could tell. We will help get it cleaned up in the morning, and you guys can do a walk-around-and-through to assess if there is any other damage we may have missed."

"And Seven Sweets?" I asked, relieved that The Alchemist was safe.

"Seven Sweets wasn't even touched. I saw Deidra before I left for home. She said she slept at your house last night, and all is well there. She also said that Theo and Tara, to her knowledge, were there with her all night."

"Oh my gosh," I said, the words coming out with a sigh. I could feel my shoulders begin to relax from their positions beside my ears.

"I have to ask, did you threaten Cliff?"

"Seriously?" I asked, immediately annoyed. I didn't want this Harrison—Detective Harrison—right now. "A. I was with you last night. B. I don't even know where Cliff lives. C. Cliff threatened us at the Ostara Festival! He said we should 'watch our backs and leave town.' I mean, do I have to put this all together?"

He looked stunned for a second, like I had slapped him across the mouth. His face dropped, and he pinched the bridge of his nose. "Okay, since we're making lists. A. No, you don't. I can handle it. B. Why didn't you tell me Cliff threatened you?"

"Why? So, I can have my 'detective boyfriend' like… beat him up? What do you mean? We already told the police about the trespassing and the letter."

"So, I'm your boyfriend?"

"Is this what you're taking away from this discussion? You know what I mean."

He slouched down onto the couch, exhausted, motioning for me to come sit by him. I did, and he pulled the blankets up over us and then my legs and feet up and over onto his lap.

"You can't blame me for trying." He grinned at me. "And calm down, Treasure. I don't believe Cliff, for the record. So, I guess Cliff has cameras all over and around his house. That's probably a relic of his criminal days—"

"So, those days are over?" I demanded to know. When would Cliff get his comeuppance? How was he not charged in relation to any of the money-laundering and general tomfoolery that was going on in Seven Hills last year? Was this truly how slowly the justice system moved?

"Of course not. But he was all excited. He said he had everything on camera with timestamps. I guess it's some service he pays for. You can see all the different camera angles on this app on his phone. Then, he turns the footage over for Chief Dodd to watch with him. I guess Chief said he can see Cliff reacting, looking stunned, looking scared, in his bedroom, just before the time he calls the police.

But then, on the camera outside of his bedroom window, on the lawn, by the house, nobody was there. Nobody in frame, nobody where he said you all were. Nothing but him reacting in the bedroom, and then, outside, the yard and the house next to him. He said they even watched the camera outside sped up for hours before and after the call he made to the police, and no matter how many times he tried to find any footage of the three of you, there wasn't any. Not anywhere on the property."

"So, what, he was like… acting in his bedroom? Pretending to be scared by something?" I asked, confused by this information. "Did he think that would work?"

"I guess," Harrison responded, rubbing my legs under the blanket, over his lap. "Chief said it was the weirdest thing he's ever seen in his entire 30-plus years on the force. Just Cliff acting frightened in his bedroom in one frame, and absolutely nothing going on outside in any other. And, like I said, they looked through hours of this footage. Nothing. Literally, nothing unusual in any frame but one solitary stray black cat."

A black cat. One solitary stray black cat. I could feel myself starting to relax a bit. Everyone could see now that Cliff was completely and utterly full of it. It sounded like his "proof" backfired massively. *Why even show the footage, knowing nothing would be there?* I wondered. But then, Cliff never was the smartest.

"Listen, Treasure," Harrison started, sounding almost professional now. Detective Harrison mode again. "We have to be careful. I can't lose my job, and you are a part of this whole debacle."

"How am I part of this?" I demanded, sweeping my legs off him in one swift motion, taking the blankets with me. "Cliff accuses me of stalking and threatening him, although we know it's been the other way around and now, somehow, I'm involved with this?"

"Stop. Stop. Stop," Harrison said, reaching for me and then stopping, perhaps thinking better of it, his hands extended in midair. He dropped them both into his lap. "You aren't involved in this. You're right. You've been staying out of it. I just need you to lie low for a bit. Stay away from Cliff. All of that…"

"Cliff came to *my* house. Cliff came to *my* booth. Now Cliff and his group of… bigots decided to head downtown to wreck *my* store, and I should stay away from him? What the hell kind of logic is this? Wow, Harrison, this is positively *puritanical* of you."

"You're right," he said, hands up, as if I had pointed a tiny pistol at him. "I'm sorry.... Listen, I'm sorry. I just meant do your best to avoid him for now... even though I know it's him. Not you. I just don't want to be dismissed from this case. I want to keep being your 'detective boyfriend,'" he teased, using air quotes around 'detective boyfriend,' leaning towards me, grinning mischievously. "That's all. It came out wrong. I'm sorry. I really am."

"Okay," I offered, my anger deflating a bit. "I can do that. I don't want to be involved. I've been staying far away and minding my own business."

"I know," he said, taking my hand. "I know you have. I just want this to be over." He released my hand then, and put his head in his hands, elbows on his lap. I scooted closer to him, rubbing his back lightly, trailing my nails over his back, feeling his scars through his buttoned-down shirt.

"I'm sorry," I said so lightly, it was a whisper. "You'll find her. I know you will."

Harrison looked up and over at me, the hopelessness written plainly across his face. "No Treasure," he responded, a dark laugh escaping his lips. "We aren't going to. It's too late." He paused and shifted back on the couch, stretching, putting his arms up behind his head, cradling his skull. "What I don't understand is how someone can just disappear."

"No one just disappears," I blurted out, and I could feel my bones turn to lead in my body. I suddenly felt heavy. Sick. Like the message I got deep in my gut about Cliff hours before, I knew this to be true. It was not possible for someone to just disappear.

Theo texted me to come home around 8 am. Harrison and I had barely slept. We laid on his leather couch, surrounded by the Culpepper Manor blankets and pillows, watching reruns. Occasionally, we would doze off only to be woken up by a particularly loud commercial featuring Chuck Norris and the Bo Flex.

"I'm leaving," I told him, shaking him slightly, after reading Theo's text message.

"No, no, don't go yet," he begged, sleepily, grabbing the arm I was shaking him with. "Stay."

"I can't," I explained, regretfully, wanting to jump back in bed and spend the entire day under the covers, "I have to feed my cat."

"Okay. But this sounds like an 'I have to wash my hair' excuse," he accused tiredly, after looking at his phone. "Just be careful. Stay at home if you can. I'm going to go downtown in a bit to assess the damage."

I nodded. "I'm careful." I gave his arm a squeeze and let go. My sisters needed me home.

When I reached Culpepper Manor, the black cat from the night I "found" the little gold key was lying on the portico before the front door. It "meowed"

loudly, as if chastising me, showing me its tiny white fangs.

"Here kitty, kitty," I said, clicking my tongue, as I stepped onto the porch. I bent down and tapped a part of the walkway, hoping it would saunter its way over to me and away from the front door. The cat did not move. Finally, I stood, moved towards the door, and then squatted right beside the animal, surprisingly clean for living outside, and stroked its tiny, bony back. "Good kitty." I said, before attempting to pick it up. Surprisingly, the cat allowed me to scoop it up into my arms and carry it into Culpepper Manor. "You need food," I murmured into its soft, pink, fuzzy, ear. The animal melted into my neck.

Theo and Tara were both in the sitting room when I entered. "Good morning," I greeted half-heartedly. "This is the cat I was telling you about."

Tara stood from where she was sitting and came over to rub the cat's head and ears. "It's very cute," she said.

"I'm glad you think so," I told her, "Because, I think it lives here now."

"So, Treasure…" Theo started, cutting to the chase. I physically stopped myself from rolling my eyes. *We can't have one moment?* "I'm assuming you know, because Travis told us you were at Detective Harrison's last night… which is a whole 'what the hell'… that some damage was done to The Alchemist last night. Luckily, the store front is mostly just dirty and nothing was broken. But, he says he thinks we should maybe stay home this morning, or at the very least, stay away from The

Alchemist. They have people there now cleaning it up. He said he will call us when they are done so we can walk around the store to assess if any other damage was done."

I nodded, clutching the cat, petting her soft fur. I guess I just decided the small animal was a girl, not even bothering to check. "I heard. Did he also tell you that Cliff accused us of trespassing on his property, standing outside his bedroom window, and threatening him?"

Theo nodded. "He did."

"Well, what he might not have told you is that apparently Cliff took in some video evidence of our 'crimes' to the station. It turns out, however, we weren't actually in any of the videos."

"Oh my gosh!" Tara exclaimed and laughed. "He is such a moron!"

"So, what Harrison told me was that Cliff took in the footage from all his cameras to the station for Chief Dodd to look at. While you can see Cliff reacting to our 'trespassing' and 'stalking' in one frame, pretending to be freaked out by the window in his bedroom, we are, of course, nowhere on the property."

"And he thought this would work to his advantage?" Theo questioned with a smirk. "Let me get this straight, he brought in proof to the police station that he was lying? That we weren't there?"

"That's right," I confirmed, now laughing with Tara.

"Maybe, he'll get on that show *'World's Dumbest Criminals'*," Tara shrieked, howling again, and Theo and I couldn't help but continue to laugh along with her. It was all so ridiculous.

"Yes, Harrison said the only thing the footage from outside showed was a lone black cat... for hours..." I laughed again, and it felt good to have some levity right now.

"A lone black cat..." Theo muttered, cocking her head to the side, looking deep in thought.

"Yes. Like our new cat. Like our new pretty-kitty," I said, nuzzling my nose into the dark fur of the cat in my arms.

"Yes, just like our new cat," Theo stated. She paused for several moments. "Do you think it's possible Cliff *did* see us? Or, at the very least, *thought* he saw us?"

"What do you mean?" Tara asked, looking skeptical. She reached her arms out and took the cat from me, nuzzling it into her chest. "I think its way more likely he made it all up to try to get us in trouble."

"The spell," Theo posed, looking emboldened. "We did a spell, and Cliff got a message from us, threatening him. Frightening him."

Now, my brain was whirling. Could it be possible Cliff thought he did—or potentially did—see us, outside of his window, as Theo was suggesting? Could 'our presence' have scared him so badly he reacted and called the police? Could that be why he took his footage to the police? Was he confident we would be there, caught on tape? Maybe he was shocked that we were not found anywhere on camera, no matter how many times they fast forwarded and rewound. Maybe the fear in his bedroom wasn't an act after all. Maybe it was real.

"The cat showed up at my last spell," I stated, making the connections. "Was this the cat at Cliff's house?" I pointed to the cat in Tara's arms for them to look at, as if they might be able to confirm. "Okay. Okay. This is all impossible, right?"

I looked to Theo and Tara for answers. We were all talking crazy. There is no way that any of this was possible. Theo and Tara looked at me and then at each other.

"The key spell worked," Tara began. "So maybe the protection spell also worked?"

"Incredible," Theo said so softly, it was a whisper.

"If both of those spells worked, does it mean we can do other things?" I asked suddenly, the world possessing stunning new possibilities.

"What other things might we be able to do? To find?" Tara implored.

"Maybe Jasper?" Theo posed, tentatively, and chills ran down my arms. "What if we could find Jasper? Know the truth? End all of this once and for all."

I considered this. Suppose we could use the locator spell to find a person? Harrison popped into my head, his beautiful head in his hands in defeat, his dilemma with Jenna. Maybe it wasn't too late to find her—or at the very least—to know the truth about what happened to her. If I was in Jenna's shoes, lost, missing, likely taken, wouldn't I want people to do anything they could to find me? Even if the methods were a bit... unorthodox?

"What about Jenna Bishop?" I questioned, breathlessly. "Could we try to locate her?"

"Then what do we do?" Tara asked, darkly. "Walk into the police station and tell them, 'Hey! We do know where she disappeared to after all!' That doesn't look suspicious. It's giving 'Cliff and the video evidence' vibes."

"But what if she needs our help?" Theo asked. "If we can, we need to do anything in this world to help this little girl. What if she is in danger?"

"We could give an anonymous tip," I suggested. "You know… if we do get a 'hit' or whatever. Or maybe talk to just Chief Dodd? He trusts us… I think."

"Or you could talk to Harrison when you drive over there in the middle of the night tonight," Tara remarked, smirking at me. "That's considering that either of you talk to each other at all."

"As opposed to the witty repartee that goes on between you and one of the goons from your dating apps?" I fired back, becoming annoyed.

"Enough!" Theo commanded, sounding a bit exhausted. "We are going to attempt the spell for Jenna. The least we can do is try to help if we can. Treasure, call Deidra."

"Why?" I asked her.

"We need a fourth."

While we waited for Deidra, we gathered all the items needed for the locator spell. When she arrived, we were all waiting for her in what was now the "spell room."

"Is this going to be... like... a regular thing?" she asked, as she entered the room.

"I'm afraid it's looking that way," Theo exclaimed, exasperated, looking a bit embarrassed. "But, I do promise we will try not to do two spells in a 24-hour period."

The cat rubbed against Deidra's leg, and she bent down to stroke its tiny head.

"The cat can be in here?" she asked.

"Of course," Theo responded, as if Deidra should have known this already.

"What if the cat breaks the circle?" she questioned.

"Cats are very spiritual animals," Theo answered. "They will not break the circle. Plus, I'm starting to think that this cat is... special."

A familiar, I thought, silently agreeing with Theo.

"I see," Deidra said, sounding a bit skeptical. "Does it have a name?"

We all pondered this for a moment.

"Daisy," I announced. "Her name is Daisy." A beautiful black cat named after Edith Daisy. It felt right.

"Alright, should we do this?" Tara asked, impatiently.

Do it, we shall. Just as we did the night before, we each removed our clothing and began the process of casting the circle. We invited in all Deities and banished negativity. Inside the circle, we were free of what oppressed us. Inside the circle, we did harm to none, as none may do harm to us. We entered into our meditation. Almost as soon as I shut my eyes, my ears begin to throb, a soft pressure that faded in and out. Instead of the bright sunny day of last night, I was in Harrison's bare apartment, on his brown leather couch, my naked back firmly pressed onto a cushion. I could feel the fabric on my back, underneath my bottom, on the backs of my legs. I sensed each point of contact all the way down to my heels, the leather as smooth as butter. I looked down, and Harrison was there. His dark head moving in between my legs, in between my thighs. He paused in his task, looked up at me, and smiled. "Such a pretty kitty," he purred.

I shook my head, trying to remove the image, and another one came crashing through. I was in a long hallway. It was the hallway of Harrison's apartment. Again, I smelled cat. And then, I felt a cat, a furball tangling its way around my ankles as I walked along. The longer I walked, the longer the hall appeared to get. I could hear the chanting. I could hear Edith Daisy's spell, and I began to run, the cat not far behind me, the hallway expanding and contracting as I went, the walls a twin throbbing to the one in my ears.

Finally, I made a turn, and I could see the outdoors. I could see trees. It was the woods. I could hear it, alive—birds chirping, the sounds of insects, the gentle rustle of the wind through the trees. I sprinted towards the opening, crashing into a gate just before I could reach it.

"Shit," I muttered, feeling the pain shoot through my body. I looked down, and I saw blood on my naked shins and blood on a white, picket gate planted in front of me. I felt faint for a moment, hating the sight, and needing the throbbing to stop.

"Stop, stop, stop!" I screamed, covering my ears with my hands. I dropped to my knees, and the hallway behind me disappeared. I was alone in the woods now, Harrison's apartment long gone. The gate was still positioned in front of me. The throbbing stopped.

"You can't come in, Treasure," A voice sounded, "You've come as far as you can."

I spun around in all directions, looking into the woods, into the trees, looking for where the voice could be coming from.

"I'm looking for a girl," I said to the voice. "Jenna Bishop."

"You can use your other gifts," the voice explained. "But you cannot come further."

A woman appeared. An older woman. Thick. Short. Nude. She had long gray hair tied into a ponytail that stretched down her back. Her energy was a bright sun that I wanted to bask in. She was familiar, but I could not place her.

"Why can't I?" I asked, breathless from the running.

"You've forgotten your Gods and Goddesses. Come back when you remember. The Craft is nothing without honoring them."

"A girl is in danger," I tried. "I have to find her."

"Worry not. She and her baby are safe."

With that, I was plunged into blackness. In the blackness, I felt around. I touched slimy wood. I was in a cabin—or more accurately—a shed. I moved around the space. Someone was living here. I tried to take my time. A table. A soft couch. The back felt broken, pushed out from years and years of use. The smell of urine, of unshowered human, of unseen body parts assaulted my nostrils. The smell of sickly-sweet perfume wafted through the air, some sweet raspberry concoction, likely meant to cover the stench of an unwashed body.

I concentrated. I smelled the woods, I smelled trees. There was the faint smell of Ozium, a chemical used to create that "new car" smell. I watched a documentary on it once—a lazy Saturday night in which I was too tired to change the channel. I breathed in again, trying to concentrate. There was also the faint smell of marijuana. A generational smell, engrained in the wood from years and years of indoor use. The type of smell that would get stronger if you took a sponge to the walls. And then a faint scent—the smell of synthetic apples. Synthetic vanilla and apples, burnt. Like a candle. One that would be marketed as a "fall favorite," but really reeked of chemicals in a jar. I heard movement. Someone was with me in the dark. I tried not to panic. I tried to settle down my breathing.

"Jenna?" I tried, but there was no answer.

I was being pulled away from the shed, from the darkness. "Treasure! Treasure!" I heard my name being called.

"Jenna?" I tried again, making an effort to stay where I was.

"Who's there?" a young voice cried. I could sense her panic, could hear her heart beating in her chest in the darkness.

The Magician

I was on the floor inside the circle, in our freshly consecrated spell room; Theo, Tara and Deidra standing over me.

"Treasure? Are you okay?" Tara shrieked.

"You're bleeding!" Deidra added, pointing down to my shins.

"I'm okay," I mustered, sitting up.

"How are you bleeding?" Theo demanded, alarmed.

"I don't know. I ran into a gate while we were doing the spell," I responded, as confused by the situation as they were.

"Holy shit," Deidra cried. "I'm freaked out!" Deidra looked as if she might pass out.

We closed the circle, dressed, and made our way to the dining room table, still half covered in witch paraphernalia.

"Did anyone get anything?" Tara inquired.

"I think I did," I announced, sliding onto a chair at the table, utterly exhausted, my shins still throbbing. "I was in... a sort of like... shed... that reeked. I was in a wooded area with all of these crazy smells. I don't know, but I think Jenna was there. I think she was safe—although she smelled like she hadn't showered in days."

"Hmmm. Weird," Theo commented. "Could you describe the smell?"

I relayed the entire experience—sans Harrison—to my sisters and Deidra.

"A baby?" Deidra queried, aloud. "Strange. There is no baby missing, right?"

"Not that I've ever heard," Tara responded.

"And you would think that would be a headline…" Theo added.

"Do you think it is anything?" I implored. "I mean do you think it means anything?"

"I don't know," Theo responded. "But I think you should tell Detective Harrison anyway."

"So, I should say, 'I smelled this shed-like thing, and I think Jenna could be there.' I would sound insane!"

"But everything else has worked," Theo postulated. "What if it's useful information?"

"I can't tell this. This is far too bizarre. Besides, he has been telling me to stay away from this case. I can't just waltz right in there and insert myself," I shrieked, feeling tired, drained, frustrated, annoyed. I wanted to stick my head in my hands and cry for days from exhaustion.

"Maybe you could… like… tell Detective Harrison casually?" Deidra suggested, and I gave her a death stare. "Or not. Okay," she responded, palms up.

"Just go to the station," Theo ordered. "Ask for Chief Dodd. Tell him you got this feeling. See what he says. Maybe it's something. Maybe it's not. At least then we can say we tried."

I wanted to relax, possibly try to sleep for a couple of hours, but all I could think about was whether I should go to the police station to tell them the sense that I got, the potential information about Jenna.

Theo, Tara, Deidra, and I debated this for what felt like hours. We almost got as far as making a literal pros and cons list. Pro: It might help find Jenna, who could be in trouble. Con: We look absolutely insane, and the entire town and police force turn on us.

"What would really change?" Tara joked at this discussion. "They've already mostly turned on us!"

"I think we should do anything and everything we can to help a child," Theo declared.

"But we don't know if this will help..." I began. "It's extremely vague."

"But it might tie into something they already know," Deidra argued.

"Not you too," I fired back at Deidra. The truth was I did not want to go to the police with this information. I wanted to help Jenna, but I wasn't sure what the cost might be. I knew how it all sounded. Spells. Witches. A missing girl. Me, once again, inserting myself into a serious investigation. There was also Harrison. *What would he think?*

"Guys," Deidra announced, standing from where she was seated at the kitchen table, after some long minutes of silence. "I have to go. I need to get back down to Seven Sweets. Are you sure you guys don't need anything? Maybe I can pop over later? You guys could make me dinner?"

"Yes," Theo agreed, "Definitely. We owe you. Chicken parmesan?"

"Okay, I'm counting on it," she said with a smile.

I stood to walk Deidra to her car. After we exited Culpepper Manor I stated, "Thank you. For doing this. I know it seems crazy..."

She looked at me, keys and purse in hand, as we reached her vehicle. "It doesn't. I know it should seem crazy," she paused to laugh. "But strangely, it feels altogether... eerily normal. And I have *you* back. You seem happy. I don't know if it is the spells or... Detective Harrison... or what. But you seem good."

I nodded. I did feel better. More alive, energized, despite the very little sleep I had lately. "Thank you, Deidra," I said, feeling so overwhelmed with gratitude for having a friend like her. A friend who loved me no matter what. "I don't know what I would do without you." I hugged her, squeezing her tight.

"Stop," she told me, after a few moments. "You're gonna make me cry." She smoothed down her teal sweatshirt, her Seven Sweets logo embossed on it, smiled at me, and got in her car. She rolled her window down.

"And Treasure..." she started, choosing her words carefully. "I think you should trust yourself. I think you might have a gift."

She rolled her window up and began her drive back into town. I walked back into Culpepper Manor, back into the kitchen, where Theo and Tara were waiting for me.

"We just got a call from Travis," Theo announced. "He wants us to go and assess the damage at The Alchemist, if there is any. Tara and I are going to go. I think you might need some time to think about what we talked about. Call if you need anything."

I watched, following Theo and Tara, as they grabbed their purses, fired up the old Chevy Caprice, and, like Deidra, started to make their way into town.

I stood on the portico for a bit, letting my mind go blank. I breathed in, and the air smelled like lavender and sage.

I showered, ate, and watched a little TV—some show about great white sharks—on my phone in my room. Then, I stood and paced a bit, carrying Edith Daisy's namesake with me as I circled the room, thinking about the message about Jenna.

"Okay, I'll go and ask for Chief Dodd. I'll tell him the feeling I got and be in and out before anyone even knows I'm there," I told Daisy, setting her on my bed. I watched her curl herself on one of my tufted pillows and thought of Harrison, the crisscrossed lines on his tired face in the middle of the night.

I thought of Jenna. I thought of her family, going half mad with worry, letting themselves get caught up with the anti-Pagan, anti-witch rhetoric, hoping and wishing that if Seven Hills changed, they would somehow get the answer they wanted; their girl would be returned. *If I can help, I should*, I told myself, almost a reprimand. I only half believed it. I thought of Deidra's words, that I should trust myself. I thought of Chief Dodd's declaration at the vigil, "You may just have the missing piece that helps to bring Jenna home." I let those thoughts propel me to grab my purse, my cellphone, and my keys. So help me, I was going to do it. I was going to go to the police station.

I exited Culpepper Manor, locking the door behind me. I was so deep in thought that I completely missed it. There was a black truck in our driveway. A Ford F-150.

Chapter 9

I turned around and saw him there, Cliff Bishop, standing defiantly, chest protruding, at his truck. I felt a profound sense of déjà vu, and my mind flashed to a memory: last year, when he came to a diner to threaten Ronnie and me, after we learned of VanHoy's embezzlement scheme. He had stood looking at Ronnie and me, cracking his knuckles—almost comically—hoping to intimidate us. He was standing beside his truck now, like he had my car, half a year ago. No corny gestures needed to incite fear, as there was no Ronnie now. There were no patrons in the diner to run to for help. There was not even Theo and Tara tucked away inside Culpepper Manor. No one to hear me scream. It was just he and I and the isolation that is Culpepper Manor. We stared each other down for a what felt like a long moment, both of us debating our next move.

"You and your sisters are ruining my life!" he yelled angrily, breaking the silent stand-off, as he started towards me.

My heart raced, and I turned my attention back to the door, to the lock, fumbling with my house keys. I manically searched my house key ring for the key to the front door and tried in vain to shove it into the lock, my hands trembling. As he gained ground, I abandoned it and began to run, dropping my purse, my cellphone, and all my keys in the process. I darted across the lawn, running along Culpepper Manor, towards the woods, thankful that we had not had rain yesterday, and I was able to keep my stride.

I kept going until I hit the woods, ducking into a well-worn entrance, a clearing, and I was on a trail, Cliff not far behind me. He was large, but he was fast, a star athlete chasing me to who knows where. My mind flashed briefly to Jenna, who days prior, might have done what I was doing in these very woods, leaving nothing but her car behind. The only evidence she was ever there at all.

I knew the trail. My legs carried me faster and faster, deeper into the woods, my lungs pumping in cold air, burning me from the inside out, as it shocked my system. The trees whipped by me in a blur. I, largely unsuccessfully, attempted to dodge sticks and branches, but eventually gave up, allowing them to whip across my skin, across my face, as I passed. I didn't know how long we had been running when I made a turn and tripped, twisting my left ankle. I yelped in pain, holding it, rocking back and forth. Cliff appeared in front of me, breathing hard, looking down on me, a predator with a wounded animal.

"I don't understand why you all are doing this to me. You were there!" he roared. "I know what I saw!"

"I—I don't know what you're talking about Cliff," I stammered, weakly, tears mingled with snot streaming down my face.

"Get up," he ordered, grabbing me by the hair, yanking me so hard, I was sure chunks would be gone. I stumbled onto my feet, my weak ankle screaming in pain. For a moment, I felt so afraid, I was paralyzed. *I might die*, I thought, my heart hammering so loud it was hard to think. *He might kill me.*

One clear thought came to me: *There is not only bark; there is bite.* A message I received—just yesterday, but now felt like days ago. I decided to fight with everything I had. I punched, scratched, trying to hit everything within my reach, but Cliff controlled me by the head, by the hair, dragging me down so that I couldn't see. I twisted and landed a good blow on his knee, and he buckled.

"You bitch!" he howled in pain, and I knew I'd stunned him for a second. He released my hair, and I was briefly mobile, hobbling as fast I could, back down the trail, towards Culpepper Manor. I could hear him, and he was pursuing me again. He tackled me hard, and I was landed immobile, all my breath coming out in one "whoosh." I could no longer breathe. He slammed my face, wet with tears and spit and snot, into the dirt. When I caught my breath, I tried to move to roll over, but he was pinning me down, still controlling me with my hair. I moved my head to the side and gasped in some air.

"Help me!" I yelled when my lungs filled. I was clawing at the ground, shredding soft, cool, dirt with my nails, trying desperately to get out from under him. Then, I felt Cliff release me ever so slightly, his body shifting on top of me. Suddenly, swiftly, he moved to stand. I took advantage of this and bellowed again, "Help me!"

I could see Cliff now, standing in front of me where I lay, cutting off the way back to Culpepper Manor. He was spinning in all directions, as if lost. As if completely mad.

"Did you hear that?" he demanded, looking at me earnestly, as if we were in this together. Just two travelers in the woods. Us against the elements.

I pushed myself up onto my elbows, and next my knees, coughing hoarsely, spitting out dirt, my whole body throbbing in pain. Cliff was lost in whatever he was doing, seeming to forget about me altogether.

"Did you hear someone?" he asked again roughly, turning his attention back to me.

I listened, and I did. I heard someone or—more accurately—people. People murmuring. Murmuring. *The murmuring Harrison described.* I pulled myself onto my feet, letting my right leg and ankle do most of the work. The murmuring got louder, and I began looking around into the trees, into the sky. I was seeing nothing abnormal. But I heard it too, and it was coming closer.

"What the hell is that?" he demanded roughly, taking a step towards me, as if I was controlling it. I recoiled, not wanting him to come any closer.

The murmurs became louder and louder, until it sounded like we were in a conference room full of people. That's when I knew it was chanting. Again and again. More than one chant occurring at the same time. I could hear it, loud but indistinct, coming towards us on a wave of sound. I could feel the energy behind me.

Cliff looked at me and then beyond me, terrified, stunned. I, myself, was so terrified that I was landed, once again, immobile. The hairs on the back of my neck stood up and goosebumps covered my arms and legs. I couldn't turn around. I couldn't look at whatever *it* was. Cliff's eyes were as big as saucers, and his hand made its way to his mouth in horror, looking past me, looking at the wave of sound. His eyes met mine again.

"Run," I exhaled out.

Cliff took off down the trail, and I followed. We were both limping now, but he was able to move much faster than I. He did not pause when we exited the woods and only once at Culpepper Manor, scooping up my purse, my phone, from the portico and taking it to his truck where he took off. I screamed for him to stop but knew it was of no use. I limped along as fast as I could, my whole body howling in pain, but relieved that he was gone, and I was safe.

I practically collapsed onto the steps, tears streaming down my face from exhaustion and fear. *How long until Theo and Tara return*, I thought. I cleared my throat and screamed for help as loud as I could. But I knew no one could hear. I closed my eyes and tried to regulate my breathing. When I opened my eyes, Daisy was there. She lazily slinked towards me, and I watched her bony back work with each step. I wondered if I was dreaming—I wondered how she got out of the house. *I left her on my bed.* She circled a spot on the porch, and then I saw Cliff had dropped one set of my keys. My car keys.

I drove straight to the police station, more determined than ever. I thanked the universe—the Gods and Goddesses that I'd long forgotten—that my right ankle was fine, and I could drive. My body was no longer screaming in pain. The adrenaline had completely taken over. I hit my hazards and parked my car right in front of the station, across the street from the downtown square.

Something was happening. We—Theo, Tara, Deidra, and I—were creating something. Moving something. Channeling something. Finally awake to something. I could not explain or describe it, but I felt it so tangibly that I could almost touch it, almost taste it. I had information about Jenna, and I knew now that it was accurate information. I knew now I was with her there—in that shed. I could help her. I limped inside the police station like a woman on fire.

The blonde, beautiful secretary at the front desk looked almost as frightened as Cliff did when she saw me. Her perfectly lined red lips contorted in an expression of horror at my appearance.

"Oh my God!" she cried, as she rushed from behind her desk towards me. "Are you okay?"

"I want to see Chief Dodd," I croaked out, weakly, and then coughed again. "I'm fine. I just need to see…"

"He's not here—" she began, and I heard a door open, someone rushing in.

"I heard a scream—Treasure? Oh my God! Shit!" Harrison was beside me, and I knew I must look insane. I knew I had a bloody nose, bloody lips, chunks of hair missing, and I could barely stand.

"Chief Dodd," I said again, as if it was the magic words.

"Treasure, what the fuck happened to you?" Harrison demanded, his hand in mine now, holding me up as I leaned. "I'm taking you to the hospital right now."

"No, no, no," I said, and I knew I must sound delirious, but I had to get this information out, before I lost my nerve, maybe even before it was too late. *Jenna is safe now, but for how long? Did she go into the shed on her own or did someone take her, put her there?* "I'm fine. I'm absolutely fine. I promise you. I need to talk to Chief Dodd. I have information... about Jenna's disappearance."

"You have information about Jenna?" he asked, bewildered, shell-shocked. "How do you have information about Jenna?"

Harrison looked at me, bright blue eyes narrowed, as I clung to him. His expression changed to devastation, betrayal, and something else I couldn't quite read. In one swift motion, he lifted me up and took me out of the reception area and into the back, the first door on the right, into what looked like their break room. He sat me on an uncomfortable orange, plasticky-looking chair, next to a metal table with a synthetic yellow marble top, covered with a smattering of napkins, and littered with individual ketchup packets. The whole room reeked like stale, slightly burnt coffee, and I noted the ancient looking coffee machine in the corner of the room.

"Treasure, you need to tell me right now what's going on." Harrison scolded me, squatting down, looking at me at eye level, as if I was a petulant toddler. "Wait, hold on. If you have information, I need another officer here... because of our... relationship."

Harrison exited the room and mere seconds later, he and Officer Stacey Jacoby returned. I didn't know how I thought this was going to play out, but this was not what I wanted. I wanted to talk to Chief Dodd about my feeling. I wanted to tell him exactly what happened. He knew my mother, had a relationship with her—possibly even loved her. Maybe he would understand.

I didn't want to talk to Harrison, and I certainly did not want to talk to Officer Jacoby, the redheaded officer from *"the day." I guess I have a new "the day" now*, I thought bitterly. Although it was not her fault, Officer Jacoby was almost the physical embodiment of my trauma. *"The day."* The time I spent in the police station since *"the day."* I grabbed a rogue napkin from the table and dabbed my nose. It was bright red with blood when I pulled it from my face. I tried not to look at it, bright red on stark white, and, instead, crumbled it into my fist.

"Jesus Christ," she said when she looked at me. She knelt in front of me, practically pushing Harrison out of the way in an effort to examine my face. "She needs an ambulance."

"I have information about Jenna," I told her, the tears continuing to roll. "And I'm fine for right now. I'm banged up and bruised. I have a twisted ankle, but I'm fine. I'll tell you about Jenna and then tell you what happened to me."

"You can tell us in the hospital," Jacoby replied, her eyes moving from my face to down my body as if she was silently assessing the damage.

"No, I'll tell you now, and then I'll go to the hospital." I was making demands. I needed to tell them about Jenna before I lost my nerve.

"Okay, tell us," Jacoby said, and Harrison moved away from me. He looked away too, out of the break room window, as if it pained him to look at me for one more second. I wondered if he thought I had this information about Jenna the whole time. Maybe he thought I was holding out on him, possibly manipulating him. I focused on Jacoby, trying to ignore his overpowering presence.

"I can't tell you how," I began.

"You need to tell us everything!" Harrison exploded angrily; his attention focused on me again. "Treasure, you need to tell us everything right now!"

I took a deep breath, ignoring him, focusing on Jacoby's fine features.

"Fine. I did a spell, and I am pretty sure that Jenna is in a shed. I'm not sure where, but I can tell you it smelled like Ozuim—" I began through gritted teeth.

"Ozuim?" Jacoby questioned. "And you did... a spell?"

"A spell?" Harrison repeated, incredulously. He began pinching the bridge of his nose and pacing the small break room. "What the fuck is going on?" he growled.

"It's new car smell," I began, choosing to stick to telling Officer Jacoby my feeling and nothing else. "A chemical. The shed smells like it, but it's in the woods, it also smells like… I don't know… sort of baked-in marijuana. I could smell Jenna; she's been there for days. I don't think she has left. And it also might smell slightly of a candle—apples and vanilla. I think she's safe. Her and her baby. I know this sounds crazy, but that's the message. That's the message that I got."

"I think she has a concussion," Harrison said to Jacoby, as if I was not in the room at all. I was a child, ranting wildly. Mommy and Daddy must talk over me, diagnose me even. I thought of the time witches stole the manhood of men in town, and I longed for those days. I suddenly wanted to escape the room. I thought of the story about the jail cell under town hall. The woman who escaped from imprisonment in a cloud of smoke while arrogant men played cards in the next room. Men who wildly underestimated women.

Jacoby was ignoring Harrison now too, her eyes focused in a dead lock on mine. "A shed that smells like a car dealership, the woods, marijuana, and a candle?" She looked at me stunned, once again, a horrible poker face. Then, she whipped around to look at Harrison who had returned to his post by the window and then back at me. "Wait, wait, wait," she said, a little breathlessly, and her hand went to her mouth. "Harrison, call an ambulance."

Jacoby was on her feet and out the door.

Harrison did not call an ambulance. Instead, I was in his basic late model sedan, making our way to the hospital. I sat as far away from him as possible, forehead on his passenger side window, watching downtown as it passed, breathing in his mahogany scent, a fire-hot rage burning in my belly, drowning out my pain. I fed it. I threw kindling on it. I focused on my anger, my frustration, my embarrassment at having revealed myself so plainly for others to gawk at. Harrison especially.

"Treasure," he said softly, kindly, breaking the silence. "Can you tell me what happened to you?"

"So now you wanna hear what I have to say?" I jeered, unkindly. I wanted to hurt him. Wound him like he wounded me.

"What am I supposed to think?" he fired back, his soft voice gone, my sparring partner returning.

"What are you supposed to think about what?!" I demanded.

"The information about Jenna?" he shot back. "You're upset? About what? That I don't believe you?"

"Yes, for starters."

"Damn it Treasure. You're hurt. I don't know if you even realize what you said in there," he spat out angrily.

"I know exactly what I said in there. I don't have a concussion, Detective," I yelled, finally angling my body to look at him.

"Don't fucking call me 'Detective.' I told you I didn't want you inserting yourself in this investigation. It looks... odd... to say the least—" he began.

"Wait... like what... like I did it? Is that what you're saying? I took Jenna? For what? Our 'Satan worship'? You're as bad as *the rest of them*," I declared, saying 'the rest of them' like I might say 'those idiots.'

"No. I know you didn't do it, but it's odd behavior... you inserting yourself into every investigation," he tried to explain rationally. I could tell he was trying to regain control of this situation. But I didn't want rationality. I didn't want to nod and say, "I see your point." I wanted to burn everything to the ground. Perhaps, I would have my fire and smoke escape after all.

I laughed bitterly, "As if everyone in this town does not involve me and my sisters in every fucking mishap that goes on around here!"

"Damn it Treasure," he barked, his composure slipping again. "I told you to stay out of it. Why couldn't you just stay out of it? Your involvement, even if off the record, complicates things."

"I don't know... maybe because Cliff came over to Culpepper Manor, again, mind you, and decided to attack me. Maybe I thought it would be better to do something about finding Jenna before I, or one of my sisters, ended up dead."

"Jesus. Is that what happened? Tell me exactly what happened," he looked over at me briefly, but then turned his attention back to the road.

"I'll tell Travis. Send him to the hospital. I'll give him my official statement."

"Are we doing this?"

"Yes, we are." I couldn't help it, and tears were streaming down my face again. I osculated through a myriad of feelings—anger, embarrassment, resentment, pain, and exhaustion. I turned my attention back to the window, to the world outside.

"Treasure," he said, and then stopped. He let out his breath in a huff. "I don't know what… to make of you. I've never known."

I said nothing.

"I never ever suspected you had anything to do with Jenna's disappearance. Never. I just don't understand why you came today with the information that you did. I don't even understand the information. I do think it has something to do with your injury… You've been attacked, traumatized in more ways than one…"

"It doesn't matter," I said softly, with a measured attempt to make my voice sound steady. I continued to stare out the window, occasionally wiping away muddy tears from my stinging face, and, at that moment, I did believe it didn't matter. I wished I had never gone to the police station at all.

"I have a hard time with trust, even with the people closest to me…" his voice trailed off. "My judgement… I don't know… and with you I feel like it's even worse."

"What?" I asked, feeling the familiar stirrings of rage boiling up again. I angled myself towards him. "You feel like your judgement is off when it comes to me?"

"I don't know. My judgement has been off... with dire consequences. I'm not saying—"

"What? That I'm bad?"

He huffed out a laugh. "I don't think you're 'bad.' But if you were bad, I don't know if I even could see it."

"What do you want me to do?" I snapped. "Should I tell you 'I'm good'? If I did one thousand times, would you even believe it?"

"I thought about you every single day in Boston, Treasure. Every day. At least once a day. I thought about you, a woman I barely knew, was hardly acquainted with," Harrison explained, at the windshield not even looking at me. "I would be out running around, out with my friends, at work... even occasionally on a date... and there you were. You would just pop into my head."

"Well, I'm sorry I interrupted *all* of your dates, Harrison," I shot back at him. "Get to your point."

He temporarily released the steering wheel, rolled his eyes to the top of his head, and gave a frustrated gesture, his hands jutting out.

"The point is... where I'm at right now... you could be a fucking serial killer, and I would still be texting you to come over at 1 am."

"You don't trust me," I stated, my voice monotone, exhaustion winning over everything at the moment. "You don't understand me, and you don't trust me. So, what does it matter?"

We arrived at the hospital. Begrudgingly, I allowed Harrison to help me limp inside. Then, I disappeared with the medical staff, relegating him to the waiting room, wishing I could slam a door behind me in his beautiful face.

I dreamt I was swimming in dark blue waters. Under the cover of night, the water was so dark, it was almost black. I paddled and paddled, the cool water rushing over my body and through me, easing my pain, quieting the constant throbbing. I went under the water, where I was submerged, nothing but the blurry full moon overhead and a peaceful tranquility within me.

The feeling did not last long because, suddenly, I realized I was not just submerged in water, I was drowning. No matter how hard I tried to fight my way to the surface, I couldn't. Someone was holding me down. I was being pushed deeper and deeper into the water, the world above getting further and further away. I looked up, and at first, I thought it was Cliff that held me under, that gripped my shoulders. I could see his angry features in the blur. But then, I realized it wasn't Cliff; it was my mother and Aunt Elaina. I looked down to discover they had bound me by string—bright red—blood red. I tried to scream, and water filled my lungs.

I woke up in the hospital, gasping, and Theo, Tara, and Deidra were there with me. I lay in a stiff, thin, blue hospital gown; my entire body feeling like one gigantic, throbbing bruise.

"You can't sleep that long," Theo explained, a motherly concern etched on her face. "We have to wake you every once in a while. It's the new concussion rules. You can sleep, but not for too long."

"I don't have a concussion," I said, for what felt like the hundredth time since I arrived at the hospital. I had said it to at least two nurses, one doctor, Harrison—multiple times—and Travis when he came to take my statement. "I'm telling you."

"Detective Harrison said you did," Deidra said from a corner chair.

"You talked to Detective Harrison?" I asked, annoyed.

"He was in the waiting room when I got here," she explained. "He said you were hit in the head pretty hard, that you had a severe concussion."

I looked from Deidra to Tara, who was also seated, but with her legs swung over the armrest of the chair, her back pressed against the armrest on the opposite side. She looked back at me, shrugged, took a gigantic swig from her coffee cup, and then examined her bright pink manicure.

"And I'm telling you I don't. He only thinks that because I was 'talking crazy' at the police station," I responded, annoyed at all of them. "I told him and Officer Jacoby about the spell and the message about Jenna because you all told me to! Now, everyone thinks I'm crazy or that I hit my head one too many times when Cliff attacked me. But I passed the whole cognition test. I'm not confused, I'm just... a Witch... I guess."

Tara suddenly started laughing, looking up from her nails, the sound filling the room. "Oh my gosh! That is hilarious."

And suddenly, I was laughing right along with her, tears streaming down my face, pain shooting through my stomach as it vibrated. Salty tears stung each of the tiny cuts on my face. I had looked at myself just once in the mirror after relieving myself in the bathroom of my hospital room, and I had never seen such a frightening sight. My dark hair was a tangled mess, cuts littered my face, blood crusted on my swollen, cracked lips and under my nose. Dirt was smeared across my face in a pattern I knew was produced by snot and tears, and it looked like a bruise would inevitably emerge on my cheek tomorrow. I had looked like a scarecrow come to life. No wonder everyone was treating me like I needed a brain.

"Why didn't you tell us this before?" Theo questioned, smiling along with Tara and me. "This definitely gives us more context."

"Because first, Travis was here taking my statement and then, the nurses were in and out. When was I supposed to tell you all? Oh yes and Harrison thinks I'm crazy because I actually told him and Officer Jacoby about the spell. It really had nothing to do with getting tackled or my head shoved into the dirt."

We all laughed.

"Bad day to get beat up," Tara said in between howls of laughter. "It makes the whole 'Witchcraft' thing much harder to believe."

The rest of the day, I received nurses and doctors, did some extra testing, and watched TV with Theo, Tara, and Deidra. At around 8:30 pm, an older nurse came in to inform them that visiting hours were over. I wanted to go home with them, but everyone insisted I stay the night for observation. About a half hour later, a kind nurse helped me to shower and change into some comfier clothes—a set of blue flannel pajamas—that Theo went home to bring me a couple of hours prior.

I was relaxing, in the dark, watching an old episode of *Friends*, completely zoning out, when there was a knock on the door. I pushed myself up on my arms into a sitting position and adjusted the pillow behind me.

"Come in," I said, and I was surprised to see Officer Stacey Jacoby, still in professional attire, black slacks and a white-button down shirt, in the doorway.

"Hi Treasure," she said gently, "Would you mind if I came in?"

"I already talked to Travis... Officer Hodge... about Cliff and everything..." I began but my voice trailed off.

"I know. I'm not here in a professional capacity... necessarily. Well, officially, I am because that is why the staff is letting me in. But off the record, I am here to talk." She took a step inside and out of the doorway, towards the bed.

"Listen, it's been a long day, and maybe I did have some sort of head trauma—"

"You didn't!" she insisted, her arms up in a defensive pose, showing me her palms. "Can I sit?"

Before I could answer, she pulled up one of the blue-and-red-patterned, upholstered chairs next to my hospital bed.

"We found Jenna," she revealed, and I was stunned. I blinked at her a few moments before she continued. "And you will never believe where we found her."

"Where?" I asked, although I was almost afraid to know. "Is she okay?"

"She is okay," Officer Jacoby confirmed, looking a little embarrassed that she didn't lead with that information. "We found her in a shed. Right here in Seven Hills. Do you remember that old shed all the kids used to hang out in after school in high school?"

Now it was my turn to look embarrassed. "I didn't exactly 'hang out' a lot in high school," I admitted.

She nodded and looked down at her fair hands that were now folded in her lap. She took a breath and then looked back up at me.

"Well, everyone used to hang out in this shed back in the day. It's in the woods behind the car dealership, downtown. Everyone would go back there, get high. I think some kids a couple grades above you started going there for that expressed purpose. A little clubhouse for drugs and underage drinking. It's barely bigger than a walk-in closet. But it has a little love seat type thing in there, a table, everything you need to get completely blasted on a Tuesday after algebra. And, at this point, you can hardly call it a shed. I cannot believe it's still standing. I'm shocked actually. I don't think many of the kids use it now, if at all. But Jenna knew it was there. I guess Cliff Bishop, who is her cousin, had told her about it some time ago, reliving stories of his 'glory days' or whatever."

I winced at Cliff's name, and, in my mind's eye, I saw his face right before he grabbed me by the hair. A face full of hatred and rage. Officer Jacoby continued.

"You know, of course, we asked all her friends and classmates about places kids hang out now. You know, where all the kids would go, and that shed never came up. Not once. I never would have thought about it—never would have remembered it if you hadn't brought it up. The scent. You know they say that scent provides the strongest memory? I don't even know if that's true or not." Officer Jacoby was smiling, almost wistfully. "Oh my gosh, even down to that damn candle. Kids would light that after they'd smoke. It's probably been in that shed for 15 years. It's still there, believe it or not."

"But wait," I started, not completely following what happened. "Why was Jenna's car off the highway, when she was downtown?"

"Well, that's the other incredible part about all of this... the incredible part of what you did, Treasure. Jenna was having some issues at home. Her parents are very strict, extremely religious, and conservative. Jenna recently found out she is pregnant. She wanted to run away and, I guess, clear her head for a while. You know how kids think. But, of course, she has no money and nowhere to go. So, Jenna and her best friend concocted this bizarre plan to just leave her car somewhere and hide her in the shed... so she could figure out what to do about the pregnancy. So, you were right. They were safe in the shed... her and her baby... unborn, of course."

Officer Jacoby paused, looked down at the tiled floor, and shook her head, before she admitted, "You know I had to ask if she knew you. Because I don't know how you could possibly know all of this. And, you know what she tells me? She doesn't know you. She said she's never even seen you before in her entire life to her knowledge. At least not that she can recall. Although, she has been into The Alchemist. She said she purchased a few things that she thought might help her with everything that is going on. And I'm sorry to report this—but she said nothing worked."

I laughed then. "Well, I hope that one review won't deter you from doing business with us in the future, Officer."

Officer Jacoby laughed merrily, her eyes twinkling in the darkness, only the blue-white glow from the TV to light our faces. "What you did was incredible, Treasure. You were brave for coming to us. I don't know how you knew what you did or did what you did, but it helped us find her and that's all that counts—to me at least."

"And Detective Harrison?" I asked, almost afraid to know the answer. I thought of his face when I left him in the hospital lobby and shook my head.

"Detective Harrison is an interesting one. It was actually kind of fun to see him all riled up today, he's usually so composed. Unreadable really. But, today, his emotions were written all over his face."

I nodded. "And where is he now?"

"Looking for Cliff. He assaulted you, Treasure, and we are not going to let him get away with it. I'm sorry. I didn't even ask if you were okay."

"I'm okay," I responded, and I smiled at her reassuringly. "I'm just glad you found Jenna, and she is safe."

"She is. And I am too. I do not know how she was living in that shed, even if it was only a few days. I do think she would have left the shed soon. It's hard to hide out for that long—stay missing—no matter how scared of your parents you are. Most of the time, missing people aren't found alive..."

She continued, and I zoned out and back into my head. Missing people. Most of the time, missing people aren't found alive... I thought of Jasper, the jar, the apparition, the journals.

I nodded politely, listening again. Officer Jacoby continued, "And she said the shed was creepy. I guess she thought she heard someone calling her name this morning. Calling her name... from inside the shed, but no one was there."

I tried to take it all in. I saw myself in the dark shed in my mind's eye, feeling around, yelling for Jenna. Her heartbeat in the darkness.

"Who knows," Jacoby said with a soft smile. "Maybe before today, I wouldn't have believed her."

I smiled back at her, thankful she came. Surprisingly, I had a warm feeling. I felt lighter.

"Thank you for coming to tell me, Officer."

Officer Jacoby nodded, "Thank you, Treasure. I can't *thank you* enough. And we're gonna find Cliff. He's had a little bit of a head start, but don't worry about that. I promise you that we will find him, and he won't get away with this."

"I know," I responded.

"Well, I better get going," Officer Jacoby said, standing. And she looked lighter as well. Today was probably a win for her. A missing young woman found safe and sound. The best-case scenario.

"Thank you again for coming and telling me."

She smiled and moved towards the door. She paused in the doorway, her hand on the door handle. "I've never seen or heard anything like it in my life. What you did," she said, a bit awestruck. "It's like you pulled a rabbit out of a hat."

Chapter 10

It was 9 o'clock in the morning when I inhaled the comforting scents of lavender and sage as I, every movement labored, climbed into Theo's old station wagon. Theo sat in the driver's seat, as Tara helped to lower me into the passenger seat. She closed the door, grabbed my crutches, and then tossed them into the rear of the car.

My official diagnosis was a sprained ankle, some bruising, and a possible concussion. No broken bones, nothing fatal. Just a sore body and another generous helping of PTSD. More trauma to add to my collection. I pictured placing "Cliff attacking me" into a wooden cabinet with glass shelves. A place of prominence, where someone else might put their own collection—my trauma, a knick-knack like a Precious Moments figurine or a Troll Doll with flaming red hair, a diamond jewel in the middle of its pot belly.

My own resentment glowed like a diamond in my own belly, polished, gleaming in the acidic conditions. *This will be the last time I am attacked, and certainly the last—without retaliation*, I decided before Tara even slid into the back seat of the car and shut the door. Theo, Tara, and a new woman, a darker woman, made our way back to Culpepper Manor. It is no wonder that women have been using energy since the beginning of time to survive in this world.

My mind drifted as we drove. I had so much to tell Theo and Tara, but I didn't have the energy to form the words. Cold rain pelted down angrily from the sky when we were leaving the hospital, so hard that Tara and I were soaked by the time we reached our vehicle. The blue flannel pajamas I was still wearing were wet, and I shivered as I moved the car vents to perfect angles, blasting the hot air on me. Goose pimples pricked on my skin under my pajamas, but I was sufficiently lulled. Comforted. And I thought I could sleep in this car, as I had one thousand times before throughout my lifetime; the scent and the heat were the perfect combination.

As we drove, I watched the watery world drift by, and it looked like a watercolor of the world I used to know. So much had changed in a few short days. How I viewed and understood the world had changed.

Lying in bed at the hospital, in the middle of the night, I had googled a name and location: Edith Daisy, Seven Hills. I came upon a couple of social media profiles, a LinkedIn, and a yearbook website. No one from Seven Hills, and based on the state of the journal—the spell book—I doubt Edith lived to see the day of social media. Also, I suspected "Daisy" was not Edith's last name, but a middle name or maybe even a coven name. I googled Edith,

Seven Hills and got numerous hits. Turns out, Edith was a very popular name at the end of the 19th century. But in the end, I found nothing, nothing that would lead me to discovering anything more about the woman whose journal changed my life. At least not yet.

In the early morning, with just the TV to light my hospital room, I made a silent vow to learn more about her. More about Magick. More about the Gods and Goddesses who, apparently, I had forgotten. *What power would I be able to harness if I remembered them, honored them? Or, perhaps, more importantly, what lessons would I learn?*

I needed to understand this energy, this power, that helped me find the tiny golden key, brought Daisy the cat to me, helped to locate Jenna, and protected me from an angry Cliff Bishop—twice. I shivered as I recalled the feel of the energy behind me. While it had scared me at the time, I knew it was possible that the energetic intervention had saved me from a further beating—maybe even saved my life.

Maybe, this energy had even saved my life last year when Hansen attacked me. *At the time, I had assumed it was a lie, but what if something had scared Hansen?* An energy of which I was not aware. Harrison seemed to believe Hansen's account of events, but, of course, that could have been teasing. Harrison. I couldn't think about him now.

After we arrived at Culpepper Manor, and after a few subpar cups of non-Seven Sweets coffee, I finally mustered the energy to relay everything to my sisters. The details of Cliff's attack, the murmuring in the woods, the energy that frightened Cliff and me, causing us to flee. Officer Jacoby's visit to the hospital. What she revealed to me: Jenna found safe. How the information we had gathered from the spell was useful after all. My suspicion that I *was* in the shed with Jenna, the supposed confirmation she heard my voice. Harrison off looking for Cliff. I was breathless and exhausted by the time I was finished with it all. So, I accepted when Tara offered to help me limp up to my room, Daisy trailing not far behind us. I could have probably made my way up alone, but she insisted.

"It'll be more annoying if we have to go back to the hospital," she said, but I knew she helped me because she cared. She lowered me down onto my bed and then pulled the comforter back on top of me. Daisy curled herself into a ball on top of my chest. After Tara exited the room, I checked my phone. I knew whose call or text I was waiting for, what high I was trying to chase, but I couldn't admit it. Not even to myself. An hour passed, and I laid in bed doing nothing, thinking of nothing but a comfy leather couch and a bare apartment named "6B." I fell into a dreamless sleep.

I heard commotion downstairs, and I sat up in bed, straining to listen. My brain instantly flashed to Cliff, and I wondered if it would for a while any time that I heard anything out of place. I shook my head "no" and worked to slow down my breathing. It was still light outside. Only 4:00 pm, according to my phone. No calls. No texts. I sat in silence, and I heard my sisters' voices, Deidra's voice, and a masculine voice—Ronnie's voice—floating up from downstairs.

So, this was our new after physical assault ritual: invite the gang over. While I was not in the mood for company, I knew that this might be just as much for Theo and Tara's comfort as my own. I swooped my legs over the edge of the bed, struggling a bit to grab my crunches and stand. I wondered if it was my own karma that now I would have physical difficulty getting out of bed, when for so many months, I fought to stay in bed, unwilling to get up and get motivated.

I hobbled to the top of the steps and called for Tara, who helped me limp downstairs slowly. I smiled when we reached the kitchen, Deidra and Ronnie were seated at the table there, picking at what appeared to be homemade bread. Theo was positioned at the oven, apron on. I noticed the witch paraphernalia was gone. As much as Ronnie was "in the gang" now, so to speak, Theo and Tara still did not completely trust him. Paranoia just as much a part of our DNA as each chromosome, so engrained in us, you could probably map it under a microscope.

"Well, I'm alive!" I cheered, with a half-hearted smile. Deidra smiled and gave a bit of a laugh, but Ronnie looked stricken. I wobbled over to the kitchen table with them and sat. I realized he hadn't yet seen me in my new state: bruised, battered, chapped, split lip, with a million tiny cuts littering my face.

I could have tried to fix myself before coming downstairs, but it turned out I was beyond caring.

"I can't believe…" Ronnie started, beginning to stand, and then stopped. He awkwardly sat back down, his eyes never leaving mine. He seemed to consider something for a moment, his handsome face contorting in thought. But then he just said, "Jesus. Treasure. I'm so glad you're okay."

I smiled weakly, "I'm okay."

"Nothing that chicken parmesan can't fix!" Theo bellowed in a forced cheerful way. She opened the oven and the smell of the peppery, battered chicken hit my nostrils. I inhaled. And although I know she was trying to make everyone feel better, I thought maybe she was right.

Tara passed a bottle of red wine around, and everyone filled their cup with a generous portion. Deidra handed the bottle to me, which Theo grabbed. "No," she chastised me, while reaching over my shoulder. "You have way too many drugs coursing through your system right now."

"Oh, Theo, lighten up," Tara joked, and we all laughed.

Dinner was served, and we ate in a relaxed way. While on the surface, it was largely cheerful and warm, there was something underneath. Uneasiness maybe? With every bite, I was wondering what Deidra and Ronnie knew about the whole ordeal. About Jenna. About everything. But I didn't ask. Afterwards, we all pitched in to clean up, myself included, and I propped up my left leg on a chair as I dried dishes.

We sat back down for a bit longer, talking about everything and nothing before Ronnie checked his phone and announced that he had better depart.

"I'll walk you out," I declared and then corrected, "Or wobble you out. You know... whatever."

Ronnie smiled at me, but his smile looked a bit strained. "Are you sure?"

"Yes, I want to ask you about something."

We were making our way to the front door of Culpepper Manor when I asked, "Is it possible that you could try to find someone for me?"

We paused in the sitting room, and he turned to look at me. "What do you mean?"

"You told me last year that you were working on tracing my family's lineage all the way back to England. Is it possible you could look for a person? A member of my family or maybe someone that lived in Seven Hills who was closely acquainted with members of my family? Her name is Edith Daisy... possibly Culpepper. Or, at least, I think that is her name. It's possible that Daisy is the last name... or maybe even a cov—a... nickname."

Ronnie considered this and then responded, "Edith was a very common name back in the day. But something about that sounds familiar. I could be misremembering though. There are so many names. I have a lot of the historical families of Seven Hills mapped back generations, so I can check. I have it all written out in my office."

"That would be great," I said and sighed, leaning down on my crutches, slumping a bit. I was still exhausted.

"Can I ask why you are looking for her?" Ronnie inquired, looking earnest.

"Would you believe me if I said I was writing an article?" I asked with a laugh.

Ronnie laughed too and rubbed his chin. The merriment seemed to reach his eyes for the first time tonight. And I knew he was remembering our time investigating VanHoy. Writing an article was our lie to Nancy, his secretary, so that we could gain access to VanHoy's schedule. Ronnie's quick thinking on his feet when Nancy seemed suspicious of us.

"No, I absolutely wouldn't," he grinned, as he made eye contact with me. And then more solemnly added, "You know I wanted to go to the hospital, but Theo told me to wait. She said you might not be feeling up to it."

"Yes, it was a tough day. I probably wouldn't have had much time to… um… hang out with you anyway. I was in and out of every test imaginable."

"I'm just glad you're okay. I just can't imagine…" he started, but then his voice trailed off.

"I know, but I'm absolutely fine. Look at me," I said and gestured to my horrific appearance. "I've never looked better."

Ronnie laughed. "You look beautiful. You always look beautiful."

My heart picked up the pace a bit, and I suddenly felt a bit sheepish. Ronnie and I did not usually talk to each other like this. "Thank you," was all I seemed to be able to muster up to say.

"I'll check out what I have, and I'll let you know," he offered.

"Thank you, Ronnie. I appreciate it."

With that, he exited Culpepper Manor out into the icy rain.

The Alchemist was dead. Theo, Tara, and I did not all have to be there. Yet, there we were. We began the day busying ourselves with tidying, working on generating back stock, and ordering. But by noon, we devolved into lounging around, reading on our kindles, and talking. Also, snacking. Endless snacking. Deidra brought in a couple boxes full of a variety of treats: chocolate and sprinkled-covered pretzels, carrot-cake whoopie pies, oatmeal-raisin cookies, and more. We gorged ourselves while we waited for customers that never came. In my less-than-ideal state, this kind of day was okay with me. I couldn't imagine having a busy day or even one of the town's many festivals on crutches, bruised and battered.

All three of us were a little worried about returning to The Alchemist. Both Theo and Tara encouraged me to stay home and rest, but I really did not want to be home alone. I wondered if I would ever want to be home alone again. Cliff's presence still loomed over us. No word that anyone had found him yet, apprehended him, and if he wanted to find any one of us, he could—very easily. But it seemed safer for him to find us at The Alchemist, downtown, surrounded by people and businesses. While we all had been shaken up by the vandals, now that Jenna was found safe, there was no reason for anyone to suspect us, or anyone else for that matter, of foul play.

Ronnie seemed surprised when I responded to his text message that I was at The Alchemist and that we were, indeed, open. It was not long after I responded to his query of my location that he arrived. The bells clanged and Ronnie walked in, decked out in a pair of brown slacks, a white button-down shirt covered with tiny navy polka-dots, and brown loafers. He held a stack of papers in his hand, and smiled when he greeted the three of us.

"So," he said, after we all exchanged pleasantries. "I think I might have found the mysterious 'Edith Daisy'."

"That quickly?" Theo asked. I had filled her, Tara, and Deidra in on my request to Ronnie after he departed our house the night before.

"You would be surprised what you can accomplish on an office-hour day during Spring Break. Surprisingly, not a lot of students showed up," he said with a laugh. He laid out the papers in his hand at the cash-register counter. "Besides, Treasure sort of got me excited!"

Tara snorted and mumbled under her breath, and Theo flicked her arm with her thumb and pointer finger. We were now gathered around Ronnie at the counter.

"That's amazing!" I exclaimed, attempting to distract Ronnie from Tara's reaction. "I'm excited too. Okay, so I have to know. Who is she?"

"Just to clarify, there is no way for me to know for sure, but based on the information you gave me, I think she might have been a domestic worker for the Culpeppers. According to the records I have, there was no Edith Culpepper in Seven Hills or… ahem…

anywhere in your family line. Unless 'Edith Daisy' was entirely a nickname, which I doubt. Anyway, Mabel and Henry Culpepper had a domestic worker living with them in the late 1800s. Her name was Edith Doyle, and she was an immigrant from Ireland. Maybe Daisy was a middle name or possibly a nickname."

"Thank you, Ronnie! That's so incredible. Okay, so do you know anything else about her?"

Ronnie smiled excitedly as he sprawled out the papers on the counter. "Of course! I found a bunch of stuff on her. A marriage license, birth certificates. She had 7 kids in less than 14 years!"

Theo marveled, "I can't imagine."

"Thank Goddess for birth control," Tara muttered.

"I wonder if she has any living descendants?" I questioned.

"Several," Ronnie replied with a laugh. "Including one living in Boston. Her name is Sophie Holland. I included her address in the paperwork. If you… I don't know… wanna reach out… I guess."

"Thank you so much, Ronnie. I appreciate it. I hope I didn't put you out at all with this request," I said and looked up from the papers to him.

"Are you kidding? This is my favorite thing to do," he responded, his eyes glittering excitedly.

Theo and Tara went back to work—or more accurately to doing absolutely nothing—and Ronnie leaned into me conspiratorially, as I flipped through the pages of paperwork. "So, Treasure, are you going to tell me what this is for?"

I laughed merrily at Ronnie's excitement. "The long and the short of it is, we found something of hers in our house."

"Okay! That is making me think we have the right person. What was the thing you found?"

I debated for a second. *What should I say?* "A journal," I stated, tentatively.

Ronnie paused, probably noting my hesitation, and, again, I laughed.

"Maybe I'll let you take a look one day," I teased, leaning in and bumping him with my shoulder.

"I wasn't going to ask!" he protested, throwing his hands up and grinning.

"Ronnie, you're practically drooling," I jeered.

Now it was his turn to chuckle, "Let's just say, if you ever offer, I absolutely will *not* turn it down, and it may or may not make my year."

"No pressure," I laughed.

"I mean just imagine… learning about what was happening in the Culpepper home at the end of the 19th century… the practices," he mused, his voice trailing off.

My mind flashed to the key returning to me, to Daisy the cat circling the key, circling my car keys, possibly terrifying Cliff outside his window, to Theo, Tara, Deidra, and I practicing Witchcraft skyclad in the servant quarters, to Sarah Culpepper appearing in my dream, to the shed that housed Jenna. My frantic searching, calling for her, her heartbeat in the darkness. The incredible wave of energy that saved me from Cliff.

"Eeeh… it's probably incredibly boring," I responded with a slight smile.

He shrugged. "You're probably right."

By the time we made it back home to Culpepper Manor, I had googled Sophie Holland so many times, I had her name, address, and tiny photo on her only social media profile, Instagram, memorized. I even found a phone number. A number I suspected was probably a land line. I wanted to call her, but what to say? *Hey, you don't know me, but I found your great-great-great grandmother's spell book and it changed my life. I hope you don't mind me asking, but did the tradition die out with your family? Go underground like it did mine? Or do you remember all the ancient practices? The Old Gods and Goddesses?*

I sat on the small loveseat in front of the fireplace in my bedroom quarters, cradling my phone, debating. After a short period, I typed in the number I found. The phone rang once. Twice. And then a voice on the other end sounded.

"Hello?" the woman's voice greeted. Questioned really. Questioned was probably more accurate.

I paused, mentally fumbling over what to say. How to begin this conversation. For all of my debating, I was freezing now that it was time to talk.

"Hello?" the woman's voice questioned again.

"Hi… um… I'm sorry… is this… Sophie Holland?"

"Yes. And who is this?" she demanded.

Again, I hesitated. A long pause. "Treasure?" she asked.

The Magician

I hung up the phone, my heart pounding so hard that for a moment I could not breathe. *Had I heard her correctly? Had she really said my name or had I imagined it?* The phrase 'possible concussion' popped into my head. I stared into the fireplace, watching the flames dance against the brick backdrop, and tried to regulate my breathing. There was absolutely no way this woman would have any idea that I would be calling... let alone who I am or my phone number.

Suddenly, my cell phone began to sound. I watched it in awe, as it vibrated next to me. A familiar number, a recently dialed number. With trembling hands, I clicked the green icon.

"Hello?" I greeted, like Sophie had before me. But questioned was, again, much more accurate.

"Treasure?" Sophie's voice asked again.

"Yes," I replied, my voice breaking a bit. I didn't know if I was on the verge of tears or some sort of breakdown.

"At the risk of sounding completely crazy, I have a message for you. I... uh... I don't really know how to... let me explain this in the most concise way... I'm a psychic... I have an ability. I get messages from beyond... you know... the grave. Anyway, I got a message from someone who has passed... He said that you might contact me... I know this sounds wild. Anyway... he claims to be your father... Now, was there something about water?"

My phone rang in the middle of the night. I rolled over to look at the screen, my sheets a tangled mess around me. I slept as if I was in a fight with my bedding, in a fight with the world. A name appeared on my screen: Detective Harrison. The name I was waiting on if I was honest with myself.

"Hello?" I answered, not even bothering to let it ring for a while, my voice thick and groggy with sleep.

"Treasure... hey... hi... I'm outside," Harrison's deep voice sounded, as thick and groggy as my own.

"Outside where?" I asked, confused, my brain still not fully firing, a part of me wondering if, perhaps, I was still asleep and dreaming.

"Outside your house," he responded, huskily, tiredly.

"Okay, I'm coming down," I announced, suddenly feeling much more awake. Alert.

I grabbed my crutches and pulled myself out of bed. It would be easier to ask Theo or Tara to help me, but I wanted to talk to Harrison alone. I hobbled into the bathroom in my bedroom chambers and looked at myself in the mirror. My cheek was colored a deep purple, seemingly darker than it had been the day before. My lip looked like it had healed up a bit, the split less noticeable, but it was still swollen and red. I assessed the scratches lining my face but decided there are no easy fixes. I splashed water on my face and tied my hair up into a neat bun before limping down the stairs.

I twisted the deadbolt and opened the door to see him standing there. Black slacks, crumpled white shirt, looking slightly yellowed, the sleeves rolled up to reveal his muscular forearms. His face looked different, tired, like he hadn't slept in days. *Beat*, Aunt Elaina might say. But he was still gorgeous, maybe the most beautiful man I had ever seen up close. I took a deep breath, and I smelled mahogany, his smell.

"Hi," he mustered, as he assessed me, and I assumed he was looking at my own haggard appearance.

"Hi," I mirrored.

"You think I might be able to come in?" he asked, politely, formally, his eyes betraying nothing. A law enforcement officer on a call. It was then I noticed the weather. Freezing. Foggy. A layer of frost covered everything but him and his car. I shivered, the wide door letting the elements in.

"Where's your jacket?" I asked quietly, as if I was testing out my voice after a long break.

"I lost it," he said, and he smiled broadly then, that 10-thousand-watt smile. His smile completely transformed his face, letting me know he was still in there. The Harrison I know or knew, at least for a little while.

"Doing what?"

"Treasure, look, I'm prepared to beg, if that's what it takes," he stated, deadly serious.

"Hmmm," I snorted. "I might like to see that." I opened the door wider and ushered him into the foyer and then the sitting room. The sight of him in Culpepper Manor, amongst our antique furniture, jarring. A modern man in this Manor, a manor, a house, practically frozen in time. He paused and looked around, as if he was taking it all in.

"Could I offer you something?" I asked, politely. "It's not Deidra's coffee by any stretch but—"

"You barely let me come in, so I'd better not push it," he quipped.

"Well, at least sit down, you're making me nervous," I demanded, my voice louder than intended. Then added more softly, "are you here for professional reasons or for... um... other reasons?"

He snorted, grinned, and did another glance around the room, before plopping down on one of our antique sofas. I propped my crutches up and lowered myself into the wingback chair, while he watched my every move, blue eyes narrowed.

"I wanted to check on you, but I didn't know... if I should... after everything," he explained. I winced remembering the embarrassing scene in the police station, in his car, and even at the hospital.

"I didn't need you to check on me... I have people that care about me," I began, before fully realizing just what that statement would sound like.

"I care about you," he implored, cutting me off.

"I recall... as a citizen. Right? Didn't you say that once?" I teased, working to lighten the mood a little.

We made eye contact, and when I smiled at him, he hunched his large body over, putting his head in his hands, rubbing his forehead. A burst of laughter escaped his lips. "Jesus, Treasure, you don't forget a thing, do you?" He looked up again, blue eyes meeting mine, and a zing of energy shot down my spine. "We found Cliff and arrested him. I wanted to come tell you in person."

"Oh," I exhaled, deflating a bit. For whatever reason, in that moment, I had completely forgotten about Cliff, probably could not have even identified him in a line-up. All there was on this green Earth was Harrison and me. A moment passed between us, and when I couldn't think of anything else to say, I uttered, "that's good."

"We charged him with assault," Harrison continued. "I don't know... I think something sort of like... broke... in his brain.... He did not seem well."

Harrison stared at me, as if waiting for me to explain the situation to him. When I said nothing, he leaned back and stretched, yawned, his shirt pulling up a bit to reveal a strip of skin that I instantly fixated on. Daisy arrived downstairs at some point in the conversation and was now rubbing herself against Harrison's legs. He scooped her up easily and placed her into his lap.

"This must be your cat," he whispered, seemingly, to himself.

"Yes. Her name is Daisy," I offered.

"Black cat," he said, and then he held Daisy up and looked at her, studied her, for probably a beat longer than what might be considered normal. He then let out a, "huhhh."

My mind flashed to the surveillance videos from Cliff. The solitary stray cat. The solitary stray *black* cat.

"A lot of weird things have happened lately... impossible things..." Harrison began, returning Daisy to his lap, moving his tongue around in his mouth, as if searching the sides of his mouth for words.

"Like what?" I asked, breathlessly. *Where was this going?*

"For one, another 'bad guy' you terrified," he mused, his tone a little lighter now. "If I told you what Cliff described happened when he was with you... what he saw... you wouldn't believe it. Nobody at the station believed it. And you know why? It was unbelievable. Impossible. People tend to not believe in the unbelievable, in the impossible. But you know what was crazy? About his story? It had some aspects I recognized..."

"Such as?" I asked, the hair on the back of my neck standing up now.

"The 'murmuring' in the woods... he described it to a tee... exactly what I experienced here... next to this property..."

I nodded, giving Harrison a half-hearted half smile. He returned the half-hearted half smile. And there we were. Two poker players. Trying to read what's in each other's hands behind each other's eyes.

"And you know Officer Jacoby found Jenna. She said the information you gave was... helpful... and... shockingly accurate," Harrison snorted again, looking down at his lap, his fingers massaging deep into Daisy's dark fur. He looked back up at me.

I opened my mouth to speak and then closed it. Not ready to fold or to call.

"Is there anything you want to tell me... about Cliff... or anything?" he questioned, tentatively. Silkily. Smoothly. Once again, a parent with a petulant child. My mind flashed back to the police station. Maybe if he spoke sweetly this time, I would reveal all.

"Are you accusing me of something?" I huffed quietly.

He laughed then, loudly, almost manically. The laugh of a person who is starved of sleep and questioning reality itself. "You know, Treasure... I wouldn't even know what to begin to accuse you of."

If this was the 1600's, I, along with my whole family, would probably have been escorted away from the house now. If this was the 1600's, we would be caged by now. Treated as less than animals. My mind drifted to the black velvet bag hidden somewhere in the house. The cow's tongue. Of course, Mom and Aunt Elaina would hide every trace of who we really were. No one could be trusted.

He chuckled, probably noting my expression. He was sounding a bit punch-drunk, laughing at inappropriate times. "Damn. Seven Hills." He leaned his elbow up on the arm of the sofa and rubbed his hand down his jaw. "I thought this would be a boring place to go. You have no idea.... Anyway, I think I owe you an apology for the Jenna thing. I should have believed you..."

"Thank you," I mustered in response.

"Yea... Jacoby's thinking we should hire you. Fire me and hire you. Says you did more in 2 minutes than we did in days.... She calls you 'The Magician' now."

The tarot card flashed in my mind's eye, holding the wand. The promise of power. Magick.

"I have to go... I have to sleep... I haven't slept in days," Harrison declared, a little slurred, standing up from the antique sofa. He made his way to the foyer and then the front door, Daisy and I trailing behind, pausing only when he noticed suitcases leaning up against the wall.

"What's with the suitcases?" he inquired, so tiredly that I started to become concerned for his drive back to "6B."

"I'm taking a trip," I explained, thinking back to my conversation with Sophie. After talking it over with Theo, Tara, and Deidra, we all agreed that I should go talk to Sophie in person. See where everything takes me. It was the beginning of something, and I had a feeling I might be away from Seven Hills for a while. "I'm headed to Boston, actually. To meet a friend. I think I might do some traveling for a while. Get out of Seven Hills."

"Wait, wait, wait," he turned from the door to face me. "For how long?"

A bit taken aback, I took a physical step back, "You know, I don't really know yet."

"But you have a cat. You can't leave a cat," he chastised, suddenly sounding more awake, looking concerned.

I blew a laugh out in a huff. "Detective Harrison... I'm not dropping her off along the highway to fend for herself. She's staying here with my sisters and Deidra. She will have three loving parents."

"I said to stop calling me 'Detective.' It's Mike. Okay. Just Mike," he lobbied, pinching the bridge of his nose. He paused before continuing. "Well, when do you leave?"

"Tomorrow," I announced. "Tomorrow's the big day."

"And what? You weren't gonna tell me?"

"I got tackled by a football player twice my size, and you didn't call or text me once!" I shouted, a match igniting in my belly.

"Jesus, Treasure. I drove you to the emergency room after that happened! And then I was working! And I thought you hated me…."

"Listen. I'm going to be traveling for a bit, but I'm coming back…" I started, my voice trailing off. "Okay?"

"Okay," he huffed, reaching for the doorknob.

"Okay," I said again. Our new favorite word.

"Well, at least let me help look after Daisy while you're gone," he implored, his gaze fixed on me, serious.

I threw my head back and laughed, "I think you need sleep."

He grinned. "I do. So, that's a yes?"

"Fine, if it means you'll go home and go to bed."

We stopped and looked at each other for a long beat.

"Goodnight, Treasure."

And he was gone.

Completely exhausted, I made my way into the sitting room and collapsed onto the antique sofa where Harrison was just moments before, letting everything wash over me. I was leaving tomorrow, maybe for a while. It was finally time to know. Time to understand it all. My mind drifted back to my conversation with Sophie, "At the risk of sounding completely crazy, I have a message for you," she had said. "I got a message from someone who has passed.... He claims to be your father.... Now, was there something about water?"

The question had rendered me completely speechless. One lone tear dropped down my cheek, the salt stinging my wounds. There was no way this woman could know my name, that I would call, my phone number, that Jasper, my father, was gone. No way. I was stunned, my mind racing to the apparition, drenched in water, the Mason jar, the photo bound with bright red string.

"Yes," I had croaked out weakly, the phone trembling in my hand. "There is something about water."

"Well," she said softly, her voice full of compassion. "This might be sort of hard to hear... but he wanted me to let you know... he's trapped."

The Magician

About The Authors

Keri

Keri Kovacsiss is an instructor of sociology at a college in Ohio. She attended Heidelberg University (2010) and the University of Toledo (2013). The Seven Hills Mystery Series was inspired by her love for Halloween and all things cozy. You can find Keri hiking, reading anything and everything about the occult, decorating for Halloween long before it is socially acceptable, and spending time with her husband, Ryan, and their dogs, Pumpkin and Sabrina.

Lea

Lea Kovacsiss works in law enforcement as a program administrator in Ohio. She attended Tiffin University (2006; 2007) and Alliant International University (2011), where she earned her Ph.D. The Seven Hills Mystery Series was the perfect opportunity to channel her vast knowledge of homicide and law enforcement into something more appropriate for polite conversation. You can find Lea baking and hosting dinner parties for family and friends with her partner, David, and their cat, Charlie.